Before Ashley could even gasp, the newcomer shoved her through the back door of the truck onto the floor and dived in behind her.

"Stay down!" His shout was nearly drowned out by the thwack of bullets hitting metal as the vehicle squealed tires and roared forward.

Ashley's entire body screamed from the tension and rough treatment. Glass shattered, and small pieces showered her. Fighting the weight that held her to the wide floor mats of the truck, she found her voice and screamed.

"Make her stop. I can't think," the driver called.

"Drive. And have a little sympathy." The new threat hefted himself to the backseat slowly. "I think you got us out of there. Nice driving." Hands, gentler this time, lifted Ashley from the floor. "You're safe...for now. But don't get up off of the floor."

Rolling to her side, Ashley prepared to scream again, but a hand lay gently across her mouth. "You're okay. Look at me." The voice was low and...familiar?

Jodie Bailey has been weaving stories since she learned how to hold a pencil. It was only recently she learned that everyone doesn't make up whole other lives for fun in their spare time. She is an army wife, a mom and a teacher who believes chocolate and a trip to the Outer Banks will cure all ills. In her spare time, she reads cookbooks, rides motorcycles and searches for the perfect cup of coffee. Jodie lives in North Carolina with her husband and her daughter.

Books by Jodie Bailey

Love Inspired Suspense

Freefall
Crossfire
Smokescreen

SMOKESCREEN

JODIE BAILEY

HARLEQUIN® LOVE INSPIRED® SUSPENSE

Recycling programs
for this product may
not exist in your area.

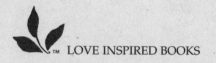

™ LOVE INSPIRED BOOKS

ISBN-13: 978-0-373-44688-9

Smokescreen

Copyright © 2015 by Jodie Bailey

www.Harlequin.com

Printed in U.S.A.

The Lord is my light and my salvation—whom shall I fear?
The Lord is the stronghold of my life—
of whom shall I be afraid?
—Psalms 27:1

To my daddy, who walked with me through
the darkest time in my life and never let me fall.

ONE

"**D**rive faster." Captain Ethan Kincaid slammed his palm on the dash of the crew-cab truck his partner piloted. At the rate they were going it would take two days to get to the Syracuse terminal. A glance at the clock said they had less than two minutes.

Craig Mitchum cast him a hard look, though his blue eyes flashed with amusement slightly out of place considering the situation. "Can't do it, bro. I scream up to an airport running a hundred and twenty, and security's going to be all over us. You want to get tied up in some back office answering questions?"

Ethan huffed but didn't relax in the seat. Every second counted. That call from Sean had rattled him clear to his core. "Someone hacked my email. They know everything. Get Ashley off that plane before they find her."

Ashley Colson was in danger she couldn't imagine and would never see coming. Even more so than on the day she'd nearly died in his arms. Ethan swallowed hard against the rising tide of nausea the image of her broken and bloody body brought forth. That would not happen again. Even if he needed to die to stop it.

Ethan had warned Sean involving her was a bad idea. He should have pulled the plug on the whole thing from the start, but he'd been willing to take any risk to catch the guys who'd killed his first partner. And now Ashley might pay a steep price for it.

Please, God. Get us there before it's too late.

"I'll swing by the drop-off and let you out so you can sweep the concourse. I'll head for the parking deck." Mitchum tapped the photo of Ashley that was jammed into the instrument panel. "This late at night, there shouldn't be a lot of people milling around. We'll find her."

Ethan grunted, convinced he could run up the long drive faster than Mitchum was navigating. In the dark of a cool spring night, the lights of the Syracuse airport bounced off the clouds, the glow painting the surrounding area in an eerie overwash. It chilled Ethan to the core, too much like the opening shot of a horror movie where the hero's worst nightmares came true.

"Kincaid. You're a ball of nerves, worse than a private in his first firefight. You're too experienced to act like this. Do you need to…?" Mitchum exhaled loudly and eased up on the gas as they approached the low, glass-enclosed pedestrian bridges between the parking lot and the terminal.

"Do I need to what?" Ethan whipped his head toward his new partner. Assigned to work with him just under a year ago, the younger man often spoke his mind without a lot of thought to the consequences of his words. It was something Ethan admired, that ability to call it as he saw it, but Ethan was not about to let the man question his ability to do the job. Not on this case.

Mitchum cleared his throat and shifted uncomfortably, readjusting his grip on the steering wheel. "Recuse yourself." The words hung on the air, too cold for the heat leaking from the vents to thaw.

Not on his life. There was no one else Ethan trusted to walk with Sean through this mission and no one else he trusted to protect Ashley.

Not that he was known for doing a stellar job. It was his fault a domestic-violence call when they were stationed as military police together had gone south and left her fighting for her life.

He shoved the memory to the side and glanced at the clock on the dash as Mitchum slowed the truck in the drop-off lane. Ashley's flight had touched down nearly ten minutes earlier. Their window slipped lower.

Sean's intel said the mission had been compromised. Their enemies had found Ashley and would be waiting. For all Ethan knew, she was already dead in some out-of-the-way corner of the airport. The thought nearly crushed his lungs. *Please, God. Don't let me be too late. Again.*

Ashley Colson's smartphone chimed as she fired it up and hitched her carry-on higher onto her shoulder. In all of her thirty years she'd never been so happy to exit an aircraft. When her feet hit the carpet of the terminal, she relaxed muscles that had been tense since the plane left Chicago. Between the couple arguing in front of her the entire flight and the turbulence battering the passengers from takeoff to touchdown, she felt as though all of the oxygen had been sucked out of that jet.

She entered the exit portal at the end of the concourse, waited for the second door to open and stepped into the main terminal. Now she was free, and she couldn't get home fast enough.

The cell phone vibrated repeatedly in her hand, so she stepped out of the trickle of traffic. No way had she missed so many calls in a couple of hours. As word of her knack for sniffing out vulnerabilities in computer networks spread, Colson Solutions grew busier, but demand hadn't been *that* high.

Hopefully, it wasn't her biggest client. Sam Mina had called her in Chicago and asked her to come to Albany to integrate new machines into their existing network. She'd put him off until Monday. Hopefully he hadn't violated their contract and hired someone else. Losing Mina would be a blow her company might not recover from.

Seven texts and four voice mails. Skipping the texts, Ashley pressed the unfamiliar number in her voice-mail queue.

"Ash, it's me." Sean's voice was low and hurried, setting her apprehension level even higher than the couple arguing on the plane. Something was wrong. "Call this number. Now." There was a hiss and a click as the call dropped. Three more similar messages amped the adrenaline in her system. Then, "I need you to go to my post-office box. Get the package from my mailbox. Work our program. And watch your back. I'm sorry, Ash. I'll explain as soon as—" A muffled shout. "I've sent—" The call cut out.

Nausea hit her hard, almost doubling her over. Sean. Her ex-fiancé and lifelong best friend.

Something was very wrong. In all of his deployments, he'd said there was no need for a cell phone in a war zone. One of his greatest fears was that something would happen to him, leaving his contact information vulnerable for anyone to see.

Knees weakening, she punched the screen to see her texts. Seven from Sean, all telling her to call until the last one. I'm sorry.

What had he done?

A force from behind propelled her forward, sent her phone flying and caused her bag to slide to her elbow with a jolt. She nearly pitched onto her face but strong hands wrapped around her upper arms. "Are you all right, miss?"

Watch your back. Sean's warning rained in her head as she spun and came face-to-face with a tall, dark man in a sleek, gray business suit.

Concern wrinkled the corners of his dark eyes. "You seem ill. Are you okay, Ms. Colson?"

How did he know her name? Ashley scanned his face, muscles tightening in her neck as she found nothing familiar. Her past bred caution and this guy unfurled every red flag possible. Her mouth opened then closed tight, refusing to ask the question.

A cold smile crinkled the edges of his lips. "Ah, see? I am more than just a helpful fellow in an airport." He leaned closer, voice lowering. "And here is something else I know about you. Your worst nightmare is any gun, but particularly one aimed in your direction." Slipping his fingers to her wrist, he pulled her hand to his rib cage, letting her fingers brush holstered cold steel, his eyes glittering above that frozen smile.

The weapon burned her fingertips, shooting fire into her soul. She wanted to scream, to run, to do anything, but her muscles froze, the memory from years ago and a deafening roar drowning out the rest of the world.

The man smiled wider, taking dark pleasure in her panic. "Your fear is my best friend." Slipping her bag from her elbow, he shrugged it onto his shoulder and wrapped an arm tightly around her waist, pressing the gun to her side, the metal digging into her rib cage. The way he held his free hand, on the strap of her bag, he could reach the trigger with very little motion. "Now, we will walk out of here together, quietly."

Some accent tinged the edges of the polished words,

but Ashley couldn't quite place it through the roar in her ears.

"And when we get where we are going, you will tell me all about your friend Sean Turner and his mission overseas. If you feel you do not need to talk, well…" He chuckled. "That is when the fun will begin."

A sob glued itself to the scream stuck in her throat. She was in trouble. Sean was in trouble. And this man had everything to do with it.

Ashley's feet dragged as the man urged her forward. The world was under water, images hazy around the edges, sounds muffled as her pulse rang in her ears. How could no one see what was happening? The late-traveling crowd trickled thin, security guards easing their scrutiny as more planes arrived than departed. No one even glanced their way.

Fear, a familiar nemesis, imprisoned her in an unbreakable paralysis. She was going to be kidnapped in plain sight. Tortured if this man got her out of sight.

There was nothing she could do, not with the weight of a gun pressing tight against her side. The man didn't even have to lay a finger on it as long as she knew it was there. A whimper broke through the solid wall in her throat.

"I can put a bullet in you right on top of that scar that is already there and be out of here before your body reaches the ground. It might be I have to go to my hotel and wash the blood out of my suit. It would not be the first time." He pulled her closer. "I would not get my pay, but I would make it out of here a free man, which is the most important thing."

"Who are you?" Ashley hated how thin her voice sounded, how she wanted to scream, but, always, that cold lump dug into her side. He could pull the trigger faster than she could ever hope to run.

"Does it matter?"

The exit doors loomed in front of her and, on the other side of the main drive, the parking garage. Despair ate at her. This was her one last chance to scream.

As she pulled in a deep breath, the man stiffened, muscles coiled. "I will kill you and anyone who tries to help you."

Ashley deflated as they stepped through the exterior doors and the cool humidity of a New York spring night enveloped them, the soft air mocking her plight. She couldn't win at the moment, but she would not give up. In the parking deck, she could hide behind a car, buy a few seconds and flag down a passing driver…though it was almost certain this man would kill anyone who stopped.

As they stepped into the dim light of the quiet parking deck, a red pickup screeched to a halt at the sidewalk in front of them and a man jumped out, blocking their path. "Thanks for dropping me off," he called to someone inside. "Let me get my stuff out of the back and I'll catch you on the return trip."

Her captor huffed and shifted his step to ease her toward the bed of the pickup, the shorter way around.

But as they stepped sideways, the man spun and threw a sudden punch, knocking her abductor's grip from her. Before Ashley could even gasp, the newcomer had shoved her through the open back door of the truck and onto the floor then dived in behind her. "Stay down!" His shout was nearly drowned out by the thwack of bullets hitting metal as the vehicle squealed tires and roared forward.

Ashley's entire body screamed from the tension and rough treatment. Glass shattered and small pieces showered them. Fighting the weight that pinned her to the wide floorboard, she found her voice and screamed.

"Make her stop. I can't think," the driver called.

"Drive. And have a little sympathy." The new threat slowly hefted himself off of her and onto the seat. "I think you got us out of there. Nice driving." He looked at Ashley. "You're safe…for now. But don't get off the floor."

Rolling to her side, Ashley prepared to scream again, but a hand lay gently across her mouth. "You're okay. Look at me." The voice was low and…familiar?

A whole new kind of adrenaline rocketed through her as her green eyes met brown ones she'd never forgotten. She sucked in a gasp, choking on the leftover scream in her throat, and buried her face in her hands, certain now this was all a bad dream. Ethan?

Sean's last words swirled. "I've sent—"

Ethan Kincaid. Sean had sent Ethan Kincaid. The man who, five years ago, had nearly cost her her life.

Fear, resentment, confusion… Ashley's expression shifted so quickly Ethan could hardly track it all. When she hid her face, it was all he could do not to pull her close and tell her he'd protect her.

Not that she'd believe him, and he didn't have time to convince her now.

Peeking over the backseat of the truck, he scanned the road behind them. "We're not being followed. Yet. But with shots fired at an airport, it won't be long."

"And with our rear end shot up, we're a little obvious. Smart guy to use a silencer, but I doubt this whole little adventure went unnoticed."

Ethan noted Mitchum's jaw was set so tight it had to hurt. He looked grim, angry. Likely because it was his truck sporting a new series of ventilation holes.

Ethan caught his eye in the rearview mirror. "Told you to let me drive."

"Shut up, Kincaid. Where do we go from here?"

Ethan watched Ashley, mind racing for a plan. She still hadn't moved, the only indication she was alive being the rapid rise and fall of her shoulders as she came dangerously close to hyperventilating. His practiced eyes scanned for wounds but didn't see anything to concern him. Not like the last time.

He laid a hand on her shoulder, fingers brushing the soft blond hair that slipped forward with every breath she took. There was no way five years had passed since he'd last seen her. She hadn't changed a bit. She was still the most beautiful woman he'd ever laid eyes on. Over time he'd managed to convince himself he'd done the right thing by leaving her to Sean, but now, in her presence, his decision reeked of stupidity and selfishness.

She worked her jaw from side to side then looked up, meeting his eyes with those improbable green ones. Even strangers had stopped her to comment. She swallowed hard. "What is going on here?" The words barely made it out through her tight jaw.

"Are you okay?"

Her nostrils flared, but she only nodded.

There was no telling what she really wanted to say to him. Right now, they were probably all blessed by her speechlessness.

Ethan tore his gaze from hers and pulled his hand to his side, the warmth of her lingering on his palm. He never should have touched her. She was Sean's. Always would be. Their engagement might have been short-lived, but whenever Sean talked about her, the strength of his feelings bled into the words.

"Kincaid? Direction here?" Mitchum needed an answer.

There was work to do and God bless his partner for pulling him back to it. Ashley might be...well, Ashley, but she was also an assignment, and she should be treated as such. Shoving the past into a box and mentally securing the lock, he leaned forward. "Call local law enforcement and tell them to step back, but don't give them a clue why. Take me to my truck, then ditch yours and get another vehicle, one our kidnapper won't recognize."

Mitchum's eyes met his in the mirror. "You think it's wise to split up?"

"I think getting Ashley to safety is priority number one. Getting the evidence is number two."

"Let me handle picking up the—"

"No. We get her safe. We link up. We move forward." One thing at a time. As long as they were in this vehicle, it wouldn't be long before the network after Ashley found them again or local law enforcement tied them up in more red tape than they had time for. While separating from his partner was normally foolhardy, there wasn't time for them to do everything and get Ashley to the safe house fast enough.

Mitchum exhaled so hard the picture of Ashley on the dash fluttered. His eye twitched. "I don't think—"

"I'm ordering you."

Ethan's voice was so firm, Ashley flinched.

She cleared her throat. "Start explaining. Now." She moved to ease up to the seat, but a sharp shake of Ethan's head sank her to the floor again. "Is Sean okay?"

There it was. The question he'd been dreading. The question with no good answer.

"We don't know." Mitchum's voice cut in from the front.

Ethan wanted to punch his partner's seat. The last thing Ashley needed right now was more uncertainty and fear. When they'd linked up for this mission, Sean had updated Ethan on Ashley's recovery, so he already knew her fear was a ticking time bomb. The post-traumatic stress following her shooting had derailed her military career and shattered her future.

Ashley's eyes slipped closed as she momentarily withdrew, sitting back against the door. Rather than fall apart the way Ethan had feared, Ashley's posture stiffened, almost stone-like in its lack of emotion. "Why did he send you, of all people?"

More than the words, the tone tore at him with serrated edges. It was a moment before he could answer. He shot Mitchum a warning glance in the rearview, then looked at her. He'd expected a panic attack, a loss of control, but she'd become a statue, an impassive observer.

The question was tougher to answer than she realized. Ethan's plan included a lot of things from shoot-outs to fistfights, but how to explain his sudden reappearance wasn't one he'd dwelled on.

"Sean's in trouble." Resignation gave Ashley's words a dull edge.

Ethan's hand twitched, the drive to comfort her overwhelming. Ashley and Sean had grown up together, even joined the army together after their parents were killed in a car accident on frozen New York roads. While Sean went infantry, Ashley joined the military police—where Ethan had fallen for her the very first time he'd seen her.

From the moment the army stationed the three of them together at Fort Carson, Colorado, they were a team, inseparable even after Ethan and Ashley moved on to Fort Drum in her home state. The hard truth was, though Ethan had fallen hard, Sean had always been the one Ashley gravitated to, the one closest to her heart.

Now her heart was in danger.

"Why would you say that?" Ethan asked, trying to gauge exactly what she knew, to stall as he worked out a plan to proceed.

Ashley didn't answer. Instead, she dug her fingers into the back of her neck, elbows locking as she pulled tight.

Ethan recognized the move. He'd seen it in the past. She was fighting a swell of panic that threatened to drown her. More than anything, he wanted to reach down and touch her, but he'd given up any right five years ago.

He turned his focus to the road behind them, wind from the broken window fluttering against his face, to let her fight her battle in peace.

It took a minute before she spoke. "He left me several messages. The last one…" The words strangled out. She pulled in a deep breath and held it before continuing. "The man at the airport let me know this was all about Sean. Now you and your buddy kidnap me and—"

"We did not kidnap you." Mitchum's voice was laced with insult.

"Really?" Ashley addressed the question to Ethan. "Then take me to my car and let me go home."

"Can't." In fact, it would be the worst thing they could do, driving a bullet-riddled vehicle straight onto airport property. Their whole operation would be upended faster than any of them could even state their names. The answers were so close, Ethan could see them on the horizon, and there was no way he was going to risk a run-in with local law enforcement that could jeopardize everything.

The panic must have passed, because Ashley dropped her hands and shifted her posture. "Then you're taking me against my will. Tell me this… It's been five years since I last saw you, since I last heard even one word from you. What makes you think I want anything to do with you? What makes you worthy of my trust?"

Mitchum snickered as he pulled into the parking lot of a fast-food restaurant, easing into the space next to Ethan's black, four-wheel-drive pickup.

Ethan winced. He'd deserved the question. It forced him to pull out the one fact he knew would make her believe he could be trusted, even though it was the last thing he wanted to talk about. "Yes, Sean sent me. He also told me if it ever came to this I should tell you something no one but the two of you would know, something he promised you he'd never tell me."

"Go on."

Ethan really didn't want to, but he had bigger fish frying than any past issues with her. "Mitchum, check your truck and pull security."

"We're wide open here. You sure you want to risk sitting still long enough for—"

"Just do it. Two minutes."

Mitchum's displeasure escaped in shades of blue as he climbed out and slammed the truck door so hard the entire vehicle rocked.

Ethan fired a silent reprimand through the window before he turned his attention to Ashley. Better to say it and get it over with than to drag it out. "Sean was about to deploy for the first time. He came to Fort Drum to see us and took you to that little steak house near post for dinner."

"Stop."

"He asked you to marry him. You said no. You got up and left him on one knee while the entire restaurant watched."

There it was. The guilt grew stronger every time he felt just a little bit relieved she'd turned Sean down the first time.

"You didn't tell him yes until later."

"I said stop." Ashley pulled her knees up to her chest and wrapped her arms around them, burying her face. "He was never supposed to tell anybody. It was…"

When she didn't finish, Ethan finished it for her. "Humiliating for both of you. I know." As hard as any of the rest of it had been, now came the hardest part, the part she'd likely hate both him and Sean for until the day she died. "He knew telling me would prove he trusted me, and you should, too. You have to. That man didn't just want to take you." She had to understand the seriousness of her situation. "He's part of a group that wants to use you as a pawn against Sean, to see if they can get him to talk and compromise an entire military operation."

Ashley shook her head from side to side. "No."

"Sean sent me because he knew you were in danger and I was the only one who could get to you in time." He fought to keep his face impassive, to not let her see he was telling her half of the story. "He's gotten into some hot water over in Afghanistan, and the bad guys are looking for any way to get to him. Including you. He doesn't have any family, and you're the closest thing he's got. It didn't take them long to track you down." Not to mention, Sean and Ethan had inadvertently pointed them right to her. It was a bad idea from the start. Right now, he just needed her to trust him enough to get them both to safety. And if he told her everything up front, there was no telling what Ashley would do. She for sure wouldn't trust him to get her out of this situation, and she'd probably never turn over the evidence she didn't even know she held.

TWO

Bullets had been fired. At her.

The seat belt clicked as Ashley shoved it into place, but the sound was a thousand miles away. She hated this sensation, the feeling she was two paces behind, both participating in and watching a movie she couldn't quite follow. It was the feeling that usually preceded a loss of control nothing could stop.

A few feet from his truck, Ethan and his partner were engaged in a heated, hand-waving discussion. Ethan seemed to be gaining the upper hand, his stance suggesting authority. It was a posture she'd seen more than once, his shoulders back, broad under the black fleece he wore, blue-jeaned legs just far enough apart to keep him from wavering. He'd filled out, grown not broader but definitely more solid, the line of his jaw sharper, more determined. He'd been dangerous enough before, but with this new maturity, he could devastate her if she let him.

With a final string of words Ashley was grateful she couldn't hear, Mitchum stalked into the darkness, leaving Ethan by himself.

Ethan climbed into his truck and turned the key.

Ashley shouldn't have agreed to go with him, should have insisted he take her to her car and give her her life back, but the implications of what had happened pressed in. The man at the airport had not only wanted her, he'd wanted to use her to hurt Sean. Ashley was a pawn to him, easily manipulated and eradicated if it furthered his agenda. She tugged her lips between her teeth, then thought better of it when pain pulsed through her skin.

She refused to wince. Somehow being insecure in the face of Ethan's confidence seemed like the worst possible thing. And blowing up in a full panic attack in front of him? Not an option. Years ago he'd left her because she was weak.

She dug her nails into her thigh and tried to hang on, to keep her body and her mind from bolting out of control. It wasn't easy with her pulse stuttering and a thin sheen of cold sweat coating her skin.

Even with Ethan's knowledge of Sean's first proposal, Ashley didn't know what to think. She had no idea what Sean was involved in or what Ethan's plans for her were.

Until Ethan proved his intentions, she wasn't about to go along without more than a story that needed to stay in the past. "You're speculating a lot. Maybe the man was trying to help me." Not likely, since he'd made his threats quite clear, but if that was the case, there was no reason to panic. Maybe—*please, Lord*—this was all some giant mistake.

Ethan's face hardened like cut stone, dark eyes steely under blond hair just long enough to have a wave in it. He checked for traffic and accelerated onto the highway. "Stop it. This is not a game." The leather seat protested as Ethan pushed against it. "You and I both know what he wanted. He threatened you. He was no Good Samaritan." The look he fired at her was one usually reserved for suspects under arrest. "Fine. Here it is. All of my cards, on the table, so you'll know this is bigger than all of us."

In that moment Ashley knew. She knew what she'd always suspected, knew there was more to his disappearance than her inability to cope with life. Her fingers balled. "You went into Intelligence."

A frown creased Ethan's cheek and he turned his attention to the road, almost as though it was too painful to look her in the eye. "I did. For a while."

Yeah, he ought to be afraid to look at her. After serving as an MP, Ashley's goals had curved toward Intelligence, gathering information on their enemies using her beloved computers. Ethan had been right there beside her, driving toward the same dream.

And Ethan had been there the day the dream blew away on the wind.

"That's why you took off when I was recovering. When I got in, you were wait-listed." The realization pounded tension across her forehead. "When I got shot, you took my spot."

"They offered me the schooling and I took it before I fully realized what was going on. If I hadn't gone in your place, someone else would have." He dragged a hand through his hair. "Sean filled me in on how you'd been doing. You got out of the army to help companies shore up their network security and infrastructures, using your contacts to hook people up with what they need to function in the twenty-first century." His smile lost its sadness and grew smug. "Am I right?"

So he thought he knew so much. Oh, how she wanted to wipe the grin off his face. "You're right, but how is this laying out all of your cards? Sounds more like you're telling me what I already know. All you're doing right now is proving you're a stalker."

The smile vanished. "Sean is working with me."

Ashley fought to keep her face impassive, even as her

eye twitched. She watched city fade into the darkness of the country through his side window. "Sean's not with Intelligence."

"No, but he's involved in an ongoing operation." Sinking against the seat, Ethan settled in as though he had a long story to tell. "And, even though you don't know it, so are you."

That wasn't true. Of all people, Sean knew better. And Ethan should, too. "What do you want?" The words rode the edge of a blade, sharp and cold.

"Trust me."

The simple request tugged at her the way Ethan alone could. But…no. He wanted her trust? After taking on the position she'd earned? After simply vanishing on the very day she'd decided to tell him she needed him in her life? She'd hurt Sean and embarrassed them both because she hadn't been able to shake her feelings for Ethan, feelings he hadn't returned.

She'd waited for him for hours, alone in her hospital room, and he'd never shown. Not that night or the next… Not ever again until today. He'd simply disappeared without even a phone call, making no further contact even when a complication from the gunshot had nearly taken her life.

Never. She'd never give him the chance to hurt her again.

Ashley held up one finger, then pinched her cheek between the thumb and index finger of her free hand, eyes welling with unshed tears. She searched Ethan's profile a long time. The headlights of a passing car illuminated the hard set of his jaw. *Hold it together, girl.* Ethan might have almost gotten her killed and taken off on her when she'd needed him, but he'd never, ever lied. "Okay. I believe you, but you tell me what you know before I tell you anything. Those cards? Still not on the table."

"Smart girl. Even if you're using those smarts against me."

No way was she going to glow at his praise. No. Way. He didn't deserve it.

Ethan didn't wait for her to respond. "Seven months ago, Sean deployed to Afghanistan. Likely it was sooner than anyone expected."

"He's been gone so much the past few years, I was pretty shocked the army would send him again when he'd been home less than a year."

"He asked."

Her eyes widened and her mouth opened, closed, opened again before she could find her voice. "Why?"

"On his last deployment, Sean got wind of some issues with the Field Ordering Officer, the guy in charge of the money going to contractors to build Forward Operating Bases and the like. He did a little digging and found discrepancies in the paperwork from some of the contractors. A group of locals and two companies in particular. Some of the discrepancies didn't match between live documents and backup copies. Someone had hacked in and made changes, small ones scattered over a lot of entries. It added up to huge amounts of cash, virtually untraceable. He contacted me because he was unsure if his chain of command was involved."

Ethan watched her closely from the corner of his eye, gauging what she knew.

Well, he could gauge all he wanted. All of this was news to her. Deeply troubling news in light of Sean's mysterious messages. "Prove to me you're helping him and not digging for information, thinking he's involved with the bad guys." Ashley knew how investigations worked, and she wouldn't tip her hand until she was certain Sean wasn't in danger.

"Nobody's saying Sean's in with the bad guys, but you know for us to be good at our jobs we have to keep every possibility in mind."

"There's no way." She shifted slightly in the seat, streetlights playing dark and light across her hands.

"Anything is possible for anybody." The truck engine hummed louder as Ethan changed lanes to take an exit that would lead them away from Syracuse and deeper into the North Country. Shadows in the cab grew darker as they left the city behind. "Money can turn even the strongest of minds."

Something about the look on his face didn't sit right with her. He couldn't possibly think Sean could be bought. "So you're telling me even you have a price?" She leaned closer, not quite bridging the gap between them. "How much would it take? Ten thousand? Half a million? At what point would you turn your back on the country you've sworn to defend? If everyone has a price, what's yours?"

Red heat hit his skin as though she'd turned a flamethrower on him. Yeah. He ought to be ashamed of himself.

Her chuckle was low and harsh. "It's insulting to you. And it would be just as insulting to Sean." She tugged at the sleeve of her black jacket. "Watch how you toss your words, Kincaid. You run the risk of sounding incredibly arrogant." In the face of her triumph, the threat of fear vanished. Control. Her very best friend. She held on to it like a life preserver.

"Tell me some small part of you doesn't think that's possible." Ashley opened her mouth to speak, but Ethan carried on. "You're the one who floated the idea when you didn't know what I was going to say."

"You weren't going there?"

"I never said it wasn't a theory, but he's the one who brought the problem to our attention. Unless that's a bluff to throw suspicion off of him, Sean's innocent." He switched gears without pausing. "My team believes what Sean uncovered is a small piece of something worse—an insurgent infiltration of our trusted contractors. That would give them access to bases, soldiers…"

Ashley was silent, watching the lines in the road, stomach churning. All of this was unthinkable but horribly plausible. "That would explain what happened to me just now. A well-connected group could have sleeper cells anywhere, and this attack wasn't random. He specifically mentioned Sean." She gasped. That message. Sean wouldn't. He hadn't.

"What?" Of course Ethan would pick up on her realization almost as fast as she had.

Ashley kept her mouth shut. If he wanted what she knew, he'd have to ask for it specifically.

Ethan checked the rearview mirror then glanced her way. "I'm guessing you figured it out. Sean sent you intel on a set of thumb drives. He asked you to pick up his mail, but there's one package he cautioned you to leave in the box."

Ashley nodded, muscles weakening. Ethan was telling the truth. "Sean's stationed in Colorado, but he forwards all of his mail to a post-office box to make it easier for me to take care of his affairs. There's one package he told me not to worry about. It was there the last time I checked the mail—a little over a week ago." The message. The package. The program they'd developed together during her recovery. Whatever was on those thumb drives, it would require their shared work to decode it.

She needed to get to her apartment. Sean's life was in danger and their program might be the one thing that could save him. "You have to take me home. Without the software Sean and I developed, those drives are worthless."

"You tell me where it's stored and Mitch will retrieve it."

"Absolutely not." Her trust in Ethan was thin enough, but there was no way she was going to hand the height of her life's work over to anyone other than him. The stakes were too high. That program, when fully realized, would fund her future and Sean's, as well.

"I'm getting you to safety. I've got a place where—"

Ashley's head shook so quickly, strands of hair clung to her eyelashes. She swept them to the side and focused on the moment. If she kept moving, kept planning, she'd forget the entire situation was spiraling. "You have to take me to my apartment."

"It's dangerous. Sean said they hacked his computer, read his emails. They knew you were on that flight, which clearly means they've studied you enough to know where you live."

"*Clearly* I have to go home. The program we developed… I didn't store it on my hard drive." The very same laptop the man at the airport had taken when he'd grabbed her bag. "It's not stored in the cloud. Encryption software like we developed is valuable, an easy target if word gets out that it exists before we're ready to shop it around. There are only two copies. The first one's hidden in my apartment and the other is in a safe-deposit box, but the keys to that are at my place, too.

"Sean's smart, and I'll guarantee you he rewrote the

encryption process on his computer overseas without creating a way to decrypt it on the same machine." Not to mention, they needed to find the key for decrypting what he'd sent, but that was a discussion they could have after Ethan drove her to her apartment. "If somebody's onto Sean and that package in his mailbox holds encrypted data, then you have nothing without what's stored at my place."

Ethan reached for his phone, stopped and banged his fist against the steering wheel. "This is where I wish I had more backup."

"What do you mean?"

"It's just me and Mitchum. I've got contact with my chain of command, but it's limited to nonclassified communications and emergencies until we're ready to move in. Believe it or not, this doesn't qualify as an emergency, and me contacting them with where you are could land us in deeper danger."

"Why just the two of you?" She'd assumed there was abundant help. If this was about to become a three-person team made up of Ethan, his pal Mitchum and her...

"Sean's involved because we sent one man in already and he...was unsuccessful. Everything points to someone working on the inside. We don't know how high this goes or who is helping who, so after what happened with our first guy overseas, my team has been whittled down to Mitchum and me with Sean assisting, keeping our information close until we can build this case.

"What we're looking at is a well-funded group with some serious hacking ability. They've been able to manipulate secure computers. They've deleted files we were using to build evidence against them, accessed encrypted emails and planted some pretty nasty viruses on our secure servers, all while staying one step ahead of us. We've gone dark. Sean got involved because we knew we could trust him to be our boots on the ground as an established infantryman who already knew what was going on. He asked me if he could forward those drives to you for safe-keeping if anything happened. I had reservations, but…" He flicked a glance her way and back to the road. "Neither of us ever thought something would happen to blow his cover and land you in danger on top of it."

"What's on those drives?"

"All of our evidence against them. They'll want those drives to destroy them, Sean to find out what we know and what we're planning, and you because they have no idea how deeply you're involved."

"So they're after me not only to get to Sean, but because they think I have his intel." Ashley's fingernails dug into her palms. Danger. The last place she ever wanted to be again. That was why she loved her computers. They were safe. Nobody ever found a gun aimed at them because they built a tougher firewall. "We have to get the software."

"You're right. But you're in danger as long as these guys are out there." He eased over to the side of the road to turn around as his phone beeped. He pulled the device from his pocket, glanced at the screen, then gripped it tighter.

"What?" Ashley's voice strained as she leaned closer, fingers trembling at the hardness in his eyes.

"It's Sean." His voice was matter-of-fact, but the expression on his face chilled the air in the cab. "Shortly after Sean contacted you, there was a breach on his FOB by insurgents posing as Afghan police."

Ashley's chest jolted with pain, the adrenaline aching in her veins. "And…?"

A muscle twitched in Ethan's cheek. "They took Sean."

THREE

Sean. Targeted. Taken by insurgents.

Ashley's bravado wore thin. Winning the battle to go to her apartment had dampened the fear and given her a sense of control, but as they raced through Syracuse in the dark, the temporary sense of power didn't last.

In just a few hours she'd gone from a network security consultant checking a friend's mail to a hunted woman on the run with a man she'd hoped never to see again. This didn't happen outside of Jason Bourne movies.

Ethan dropped one hand from the wheel and let it fall between them on the console. "You okay?"

"Why do you ask?"

"That was one mighty big sigh you just let out over there." He sniffed. "Listen. It's bound to not be easy right now, but we'll figure out who's behind all of this and find Sean. We have the benefit of knowing this wasn't random. We have leads. It might take some time, but we'll get it done."

Something about the renewed confidence in his voice soothed Ashley. It washed over her in the soft darkness and made her believe he was right—it would all be okay. Eventually. She settled into the corner against the door, pulling the seat belt tighter in case anyone found them on the street and tried to take them out.

But nothing could keep the silence from pressing in. She wished there was something to talk about, but shock and weariness kept her mind focused on the monsters that could be lurking outside her home. Even that was better than letting her mind wonder if Sean was alive.

Her home. Her safe place. It would probably never be that again. Especially considering… "Have you been to my apartment before? Pulling surveillance on me?"

Ethan didn't answer, but the fact he hadn't asked for directions to her place spoke louder than words. The lights of his truck played across the front parking lot and he turned them off before they got to the side street of the building where her apartment was housed. He pulled into a space around a curve several buildings away from hers and cut the engine. "If you tell me where it is, I can go get it."

And leave her here alone, a sitting duck for anyone who happened to spot her? No, thank you. Her best option was to go with him and face whatever giants might be lurking in her living room. "It's too hard to explain, and you'll need a screwdriver."

His eyebrow arched, the shadow of the streetlights making him look like a supervillain in an old cartoon. All he needed was a mustache to twirl. It would have made her laugh under different circumstances.

Ashley reached for the door handle but a short grunt stopped her. Ethan flipped a switch by the steering wheel and popped his door open cautiously. When the interior lights stayed dark, he tipped her a nod and met her at the front of the truck, hand at his hip under his jacket.

Ashley's eyes drifted closed as she wavered on her feet. She hadn't considered he'd be armed. His reflexive movement as they faced danger spoke more than words. Even though they'd escaped the airport, she was still in a situation requiring weapons. She'd grown up around guns, been trained to use them, and still the irrational, stupid fear won every time. The memory of pain and stolen dreams overwhelmed her common sense.

Pulling in a deep breath, she released it slowly. *Be strong. Focus on where you are right now.* Ethan could never know how much the past still haunted her nightmares.

As much as she feared the gun at Ethan's side, she edged closer. Right now, he was the one safe thing in her life. Ironic, considering his propensity for leaving when it suited him. Considering how her heart started to beat double-time when she'd realized he was her rescuer, it was best if she remembered that. *Focus on the soft feel of the air... On the smell of smoke from someone's fireplace... Anything other than guns and Ethan.*

They slipped across the parking lot to the back, where a few feet of small yard stood between them and the protective wall that buffered the sounds from the road behind the building.

Ashley followed Ethan into the breezeway and up to the exterior stairs to the second level, stopping short when he did. The door to her apartment stood open slightly, the wood around the lock splintered. The intruders hadn't even tried to hide their entrance. Far from fear, hot fury surged. It took a lot of chutzpah to bust into someone's home without even caring if the whole apartment complex knew about it.

Motioning for her to follow, Ethan held a finger to his lips then slipped up the short breezeway to the stairs leading to the third floor. He ushered her underneath the open cement-and-metal structure. "Wait here."

Ashley wanted to protest, but she knew better. Arguing would waste valuable time and he'd never let her go anyway. She stood tense against the wall, trying to make herself small.

No movement came from her apartment. The light wind that always seemed to blow through this part of the state whispered against her ears, blurring the finer sounds.

It felt like hours before Ethan appeared in the doorway, the dim lights of the breezeway playing strange shadows across his face. His eyes stood out, glittering with an emotion she couldn't define. "It's clear, but I wish you didn't have to see it."

Ashley's mind and body downshifted into a place worse than fear. She was numb. From the inside out, she felt nothing. The chilled air, the thought she could die… Nothing connected. She wanted to pinch herself just to jolt something into her brain.

"Ash? If you tell me where it is, I can get it. You don't have to come in. It's probably better if—"

She didn't let him finish. She needed to move, needed to feel something in her body, even if it was the simple forward motion of putting one foot in front of the other. Pushing past him, Ashley paused in the doorway and stared.

The streetlight in the parking lot leaked through the purple curtains at the front of the living room, casting a violet haze over the scene. Even in the dim light, it was obvious everything had been tossed, as though a tsunami had broken in the room and retreated. The light made the whole scene surreal, more frightening than it should be, the glow too much like a haunted house that had given Ashley nightmares as a child.

As badly as she wanted to flood the place with light, she knew better. It would only tip off anyone watching.

She stopped by the entrance as Ethan slipped the door shut the best he could behind her. "You're sure you cleared the place?"

"Would I have let you in if I hadn't?"

This sarcastic side of him didn't even make her flinch. It tended to come out when he was stressed, worried about the unknown. The last time she'd heard it was at her hospital bedside the night her entire life blew apart.

Definitely not the place her imagination should go right now. The fear jolted again and brought a brusqueness with it. "A simple yes would have worked. I want to know they're not going to pop up again when I pull the portable hard drive out. And I want to be double sure they don't see what I'm about to do now." She laid her hand against the wall and felt for the kitchen, inching forward, toes connecting with what was left of her normal life. Her sanctuary no longer brought safety. The violation fouled the air and crawled along her skin.

With no windows in the small kitchen, the blackness hung thick and inky. She could almost feel invisible hands poised to grasp her and yank her into a pit where her floor used to be.

She allowed herself a tight smile. Whoever was searching must have thought they'd found what they were looking for.

Laying hands on the small flashlight she kept in her junk drawer brought little relief, since it only served to make the darkness outside the beam even thicker, but it was better than nothing. She found a small screwdriver and, careful to keep the beam aimed at the floor and away from the windows, stepped over what she could now see. An overturned dining chair. The phone char-

ger she'd left behind in her mad dash to make the plane.
A spare key to her car.

She shoved it into her pocket. They'd need it when they
went to the airport to get the keys to Sean's post-office
box from her glove box.

The light glinted off of something shiny.

Ashley swallowed hard. The Blue Willow china plate
that had hung near the dining room table, the one tangible
item left from her great-grandmother, had been smashed,
fine pieces ground into the carpet. Something about those
impossibly small shards on the floor undid her in a way
nothing else could.

She bit back a sob Ethan was bound to hear.

He had. There was a scrape of movement near the
door. "They found the software?"

Ashley shook her head then realized he couldn't see
her in the dark. It was a second before she could trust herself to answer. "Doubtful." The word cracked just like the
plate. She cleared her throat and straightened her shoulders. There were too many things to do, too many moves
to make, for her to fall apart now. This was only the beginning.

Trying to corral her thoughts, she stepped gently over
the plate and ran her hand along the wooden lip underneath the small, round dining table. Her fingers caught
on a piece of duct tape barely hanging on to the wood at
the far end of the curve. "They took it."

Ethan was at her side before she even heard him move.
"They took your program?" His voice drew tight, the dark
magnifying the whisper until it sounded like a shout.

"No, I hid a dummy one." She edged away, cheeks
warming, even though the circumstances were wrong and
history said she really shouldn't notice. "Call it paranoia.
Sean and I worked hard writing the software, and it could

be worth more money than you can imagine. It's not perfected, because we haven't had time together to work out the bugs. Thieves want easy information they can sell. I figured if anyone ever broke into my house, they'd check obvious locations, think they'd found something important and leave. I never expected to end up needing this."

"Still with the killer instinct. You're something else." The words curved on a grin Ashley could see in her mind if not in the dark. "What'd you put on it?"

It was getting hard not to tamp down the pride at his compliments. When had she gotten to the place she lit up at someone else's approval? "Some photos my dad sent from Haiti and some medium-level encrypted files to keep anybody busy if they happen to snoop."

"This ought to be good. What did you encrypt?"

"The stats for the postseason every year the Red Sox won the World Series."

"Beautiful." Ethan was all business again. "And are you sure they haven't found the real one?"

"Not unless they moved the entertainment center." Ashley slipped past, careful not to touch him. Something about Ethan and the dark made her want to talk, to tell him how she'd said no to Sean's first proposal because some nagging little voice at the back of her mind whispered they were friends, not life partners. When she thought of her future, even now in the rare times she allowed herself to dream, it was Ethan in her front-porch-rocker visions.

Not that it mattered. Ethan had left her and Sean had stuck by her, his sympathy and her fear driving them into a rocky engagement that nearly ended their friendship before they realized their mistake. Even now she was growing more certain it was because Ethan had always been the one who owned her love.

This day needed to end before she capped it by opening her mouth and humiliating herself.

Stepping over scattered parts of her life as she entered
the living room, Ashley scanned the area. Couch pillows and books littered the floor. Thankfully, the large
wooden cabinet holding her television sat square in the
wall. She'd banked on it being too heavy for anyone to
move and, thankfully, she'd been right.

Tucking the screwdriver into her hip pocket, she crouched
so she could move the cabinet, back braced against wood,
legs providing the force. But after the rush of the day, her
muscles weren't ready to cooperate. "C'mon." She gestured
between Ethan and the cabinet. "Put your muscles into it."

He leaned back, his shoulder brushing hers, sliding
against the cabinet to get his body into position. "Can't
wait to see where this is going."

"About six inches to the right. Now push."

The bulk of the cabinet hesitated then slid in the dark,
gaining momentum as it moved.

"Nice job." Ashley guided Ethan out of the way and
knelt in front of the wall outlet. Popping the small flashlight between her teeth, she pulled out the screwdriver
and removed the outlet cover from the wall.

"You have got to be kidding me." Ethan knelt behind
her.

His breath tickled her hair. Her hands stilled, the plastic cover weightless in her fingers. For a moment she
wanted to lean into him, to let him support her, to forget
this whole wretched day ever happened, to pretend he
was still the same Ethan and five years hadn't changed
them. The outlet cover slipped from her fingers, the motion jolting her into the moment. They didn't have time
to waste. If anyone was watching her apartment, they
knew Ethan and Ashley were there and wouldn't hesi-

tate to return, especially if they believed she possessed Sean's intel.

"How did you keep the electricity from wiping out the drive?" Ethan leaned closer, curiosity overtaking his sense of propriety.

"That's a remote possibility, but it's not in the outlet." Ashley made quick work of two more screws and slipped the entire socket from the wall, exposing the hole where the outlet slid into place. "It's between the walls." She reached in with two fingers, found the duct tape attaching the small portable drive to the inside of the drywall and pulled it free. "There you have it."

"I'll have to remember that one." Ethan eased to his feet and held a hand out to help her up. Ashley hesitated before she took it and then let him pull her to her feet, dropping his hand as quickly as she could steady herself. "Let's go before they get too deep into your dummy files and figure out you've skunked them with your secret squirrel self, although I think it's going to take some time for them to figure out they're looking at Big Papi's stellar season."

"Here's hoping."

In the dim light Ethan's gaze captured hers. "You'd have been a real asset to—" He broke the moment, stepping toward the door. "We need to get moving."

They were mere feet from the door when a scrape and a man's whisper leaked around the damaged frame. "Somebody's in there."

Ashley froze as Ethan stepped protectively in front of her, hand at his hip. "You have a balcony?"

"Off the bedroom." *With a whole other story between us and the ground.* Ashley had thought many times about how she'd get out of her apartment if there was a fire, but she never dreamed she'd actually have to dangle above the bushes on the ground floor.

Ethan shoved her toward the hallway. "Think you can take the fall?"

FOUR

There wasn't one moment of hesitation. Ashley was up the hallway before Ethan could tell her to move, and he was close behind. The possibility it could simply be the police or her landlord didn't matter. The risks were too great.

Once he stepped into the room behind her, he slipped the door shut and clicked the lock. If it was their friend from the airport, the hollow door would buy them a few seconds, but those ticks of the clock might mean all the difference.

Light flooded under the door as someone flipped a switch in the front of the apartment. "See? Nobody's in here."

"I heard voices."

The French doors on the other side of the bedroom whispered open, silhouetting Ashley against the dim glow from outside. She waved him forward. "Drop's a few feet if you can hang on to the rail and let your feet dangle." Throwing a leg over the side, she gifted him a grim smile. "Pray my downstairs neighbors aren't looking out the window. And be careful."

She was scared to death if she was this calm. Her emotional defenses drove her to a place where she felt nothing just to avoid the fear. He'd seen it on the battlefield, even experienced it himself. Ethan wished there was time to make sure she landed safely, but the lock jiggled behind him and a shout followed.

Shoving his gun into its holster, he climbed the rail, ran his hands down to the bottom of the wood railing and let his feet dangle in space. The sound of splintering door covered his crouched landing in the bushes below.

Their visitor was definitely not the landlord.

He was safely around the corner before voices rained down from above. "Nobody's here."

"So who locked the door?"

"Maybe you did when we left? No way they jumped without breaking something." The voice strained as though the man leaned over the railing to prove his theory.

Ethan fought his muscles aching for a quick peek around the corner to see if one of the men was the assailant from the airport or if he and Ashley faced bigger worries.

She tugged at his arm. "Come on. Before they figure out we moved furniture and start looking for us."

Tucking her behind him, a move he was sure to hear about later, Ethan reached for his gun but stopped. The way Ashley had reacted earlier, there was no telling what her response would be, and they needed all of her focus to get out of here alive. At this point, her emotional lockdown was their salvation.

She pressed close to him as he edged along the brick toward the front of the building, so close her warmth telegraphed through the thin fleece of his jacket. The sooner they were safely in his truck and she was a couple of feet away, the better.

At the corner he stopped and surveyed the grass-ringed

parking lot. Not for the first time he hated the even spacing of streetlights that left few shadows in which to hide.

Ashley's words tickled his ear. "What now?" She didn't wait for an answer. "There's a small ditch along the back of the parking lot." Her arm snaked in front of him, indicating a spot at their two o'clock. "If we can make it without being spotted, we can get low enough to avoid detection and get to your truck."

The pride he'd battled all of his life fought to take charge, to seize the moment and come up with the foolproof idea that would save the day. But he couldn't. The route she'd laid out was the only way to safety.

She shuddered against his back, snapping him out of his self-recrimination. They needed to move before the situation dug in and she dissolved into panic. As much as he wanted her to be well, to be his old Ashley, the little time they'd spent together had already clued him in to the fear that plagued her. He fought against the warm bile of guilt in his stomach and forced himself to focus.

With Ashley breathing against his neck and his heart pounding from the stress of the moment, he could hardly hear if their visitors were lurking. "That ten feet of open grass bugs me." Even his whisper echoed in the stillness.

"No choice but to go for it."

If he closed his eyes Ethan could fool himself into believing they were still partners, still shared the easy rhythm that let them get the job done effortlessly. But they weren't and likely never would be again.

Ethan tried one more time to listen for footsteps, voices—anything. Only the distant sounds of cars on the main road drifted to them. "Okay." He slipped his hand behind him and found hers. He wanted her close in case anything happened. No matter what, unlike the last time, he would know he'd done all he could to protect her. "Let's go."

With a quick prayer Ethan plunged out of their hiding place, Ashley keeping pace behind. The damp grass, not yet revived after the long winter, crushed beneath their feet, leaving a dim trail to their destination. They'd have to move fast once they hit the ditch. He leaped in feet-first, Ashley a millisecond behind him.

"You hear that?" The shout came muffled from above, probably from the balcony they'd recently vacated.

They had time, but not much. Propelling her by her biceps, he urged her forward. "Run."

They slipped and slid along the ditch, feet skittering on the thin layer of mud in the bottom, Ethan's ears tuned for the sounds that would let him know their pursuers had found their footprints.

Please, God. Hide us a little bit longer.

Behind him, Ashley muttered softly and he wondered if she, too, was petitioning for cover.

They rounded the bend in the ditch and Ethan scanned for a spot gentle enough for them to climb. "There."

As he said it, a shout echoed across the night. They had a few more seconds before they were found. Jerking Ashley in front of him, he hefted her up the bank and scrambled up behind her, coming out just inches from the bumper of his truck.

Ashley beat him inside.

Shutting the door behind him, Ethan twisted the key in the ignition and, headlights off, drove as fast as he dared, praying the men hadn't caught up in time to tail them. They were on the main road and two turns away before the bands around his chest relaxed. "They didn't follow us."

Ashley just nodded, arms crossed, fingers digging into her biceps. Her breaths came rapidly, shallow and hard.

He knew better than to touch her. She was on the edge of falling apart. "Talk to me, Ash."

"Pull over."

Ethan checked the rearview mirror, but no headlights flashed. Still, it was ludicrous to stop now. "I can't. They're bound to have figured out—"

"Pull over. Find a place." Her voice was barely audible over her need for air. "Now."

Ethan kneaded the steering wheel, tension radiating up his arms and into his shoulders. He couldn't. It would be suicide, but Ashley was now gripping the headrest as though it was going to keep her from spinning off of the planet.

She turned her head to him, eyes pleading behind a sheen of tears. "Please, Ethan."

His foot eased off the gas. Okay, he'd find a place to pull over.

Even if it killed them.

She could die right now. It would be just fine with her. The fact death was a real possibility didn't matter. In the throes of uncontrollable emotion, the shame burning her gut eclipsed the fear of death.

Her body rebelled, refusing to believe there was nothing to fear because, this time, there was definitely something to be afraid of. And the reality was as bad as any of her nightmares.

Ashley had felt it the instant Ethan shifted the truck into gear, the moment she knew they were relatively safe and making a getaway. The fog she'd walked in for the past hour blew away, chased by hot fear. The cold sweat… The tight muscles trying to claw out of her skin… This was a full-blown panic attack the likes of which she hadn't experienced in more than three years. One the rapidly shrinking rational part of her brain could not believe she was about to have in front of Ethan Kincaid.

The minute he pulled around to the back of a darkened gas station, Ashley yanked the door handle, slid from the truck, leaned against the cold metal and locked her hands against her knees. The damp night air filled her lungs and eased her body as she fought nausea, praying Ethan would stay in the truck and pretend everything was A-okay.

No such luck. His boots scrunched the gravel and came into view. "Ash?"

He might as well have shouted, because the whisper rained condemnation hotter than nuclear fallout. She was weak. Not strong enough. Still haunted by a weakness that defied explanation, one she should have overcome years ago.

The same weakness that had stolen her dream and laid it at Ethan's feet.

His arm brushed her shoulder, but she swatted it away so hard her hand stung. The pain was enough to drag her into the present and she rooted herself in her former therapist's advice. *Be grounded in the moment. Be aware of where you are right now.*

It wasn't helping. Right now, in the moment, she was hiding from men who wanted her dead with a man who wanted…what, exactly?

Ethan possessed the good sense to step away and let her have some space. The warmth of him left her and gravel crunched under his feet as he paced toward the road. Let him patrol. Right now, she almost didn't care if the bad guys did find them. At least she wouldn't be tormented by terror anymore.

In the moment. Okay. In this moment, no gun was aimed at her head. At least not that she was aware of.

She swept the thought away.

In this moment, gray mud coated the toes of her brown boots and the hem of her good jeans. Ashley focused on the dirt and the way it played on her boots, taking her mind out of the fear.

By the time Ethan crunched back to her, the dust had cleared from her mind if not from her feet. Trembling, Ashley pulled herself upright and inhaled deeply, bracing her hands against the sides of his truck, wrung out from the aftereffects of panic.

Ethan leaned beside her, not close enough to touch her but definitely close enough for the warmth of him to penetrate her jacket. "You okay?"

She glanced at him, but he wasn't looking at her. Instead he scanned the tree line, the side of the building, trying to keep an eye out for any possible incursions. Knowing he wasn't watching her eased the remaining tension in her shoulders. "I'm okay." But she'd be better if she were alone. What she wouldn't give for five minutes all by herself to knit her thoughts together.

"So that still happens?" There was no emotion in his words, no condemnation.

Her spine stiffened. Yes, that still happened, though not in a very long time. It was a failing she'd never been able to hide from him, as much as she'd tried. In spite of weak knees threatening to dump her to the ground, she pushed herself away from the truck, taking a second to steady her legs. "I said I'm fine." And she would be, eventually, if he'd quit focusing on her. "Shouldn't we be getting out of here?" She yanked open the truck door, even though the interior of the vehicle shrank into a claustrophobic nightmare.

This would take all of her willpower. Honestly, men with guns high-speed chasing them through the night was way less scary than standing here while Ethan realized she was still only half of her former self.

"I think we're fairly safe here." He didn't move, didn't pull out his keys and act as though it was imperative they hit the road again. "You know you can't handle this on your own, right?"

Her hand froze on the cool metal of the door. He was in no position to give her advice, not when he had no idea what her life was like thanks to his running away. "When did you become a therapist? Did you learn that when you were in Intelligence training?" Ashley winced at her words. That was the one thing she really shouldn't have brought up in front of him. Maybe he hadn't heard.

"Very few days go by that I don't think about how what I have came to me at the expense of your dreams."

"And you left like a coward without telling me why." Without giving him a chance to respond, Ashley hefted herself into the truck and slammed the door shut. If Ethan hadn't taken her spot, someone else would have, but she couldn't let it go, couldn't stand to be reminded her life was working on plan F: fear and failure.

It was a long time before he climbed in the other side and slid the key into the ignition, though he didn't turn the engine over. "Ash, I—"

"The conversation's over. The past is done." *If only.* "Sean needs us. Let's just get those thumb drives from the post office, find the decryption code and pass it all on to whoever needs them to shut your case and bring Sean home. Then you can go back to your intelligence gathering and I can go back to my computers."

Ethan's fingers dropped from the ignition. "You know it's not going to be easy."

Oh, but she wanted it to be.

"Ash, you can't go home until these guys are caught. It's not safe for you until—"

"I know." But that didn't mean she wanted to think about it. Ethan and Sean had ripped her from her safe, controlled existence. A few miles away her apartment lay in shambles and she couldn't go home anytime soon…if ever. In her swirling life, she needed a safe place or she was in danger of losing every inch of the ground she'd recovered since the day she'd been shot. "Just give me a few minutes where I can pretend none of this is happening."

"What good's that going to do you?"

"None." Ashley ran a hand along her thigh and gripped the front of the seat, the leather soft beneath her fingers. "Where do we have to take the drives for you to have them analyzed? And where's the cipher key?"

Beside her, Ethan froze. It was as if time had stopped and held him in suspended animation.

"The cipher key? The decryption code? Ethan, if Sean didn't give you a key, the program's useless. We set up the program using a symmetric key algorithm. The data's encrypted in files, but the encryption requires a key, some kind of code to lock and unlock the data. Sean's too smart to mail it with the drives themselves. Did he give you any clue where it is? Where he hid it?"

Ethan was quiet so long Ashley ventured a look. He was staring at her, expression unreadable except for his eyes. The brown of them was deep, dark…and sad. "I don't have the cipher." He started the truck, the vents blasting warm air into Ashley's face. "You do."

The heat from the vents battled the cold running through Ashley's veins. He couldn't possibly be saying what she thought he was. "No."

"I have no idea what Sean meant, but you're it. You're

all we've got, because there's no one else we can trust. He said you'd know everything once you saw the data."

Physical pain thundered through her chest and shot lightning bolts into her extremities. A sudden rush of panic and she was clawing for the door, the lock... Anything. Any way to be free. She held the key, the one thing between Sean and death, between those men and the information they wanted.

Hands grasped her shoulders, angled her toward Ethan. Firm fingers tipped her chin and gently turned her head. As violently as she tried to fight, the gentle press of those warm fingers didn't let up.

"Ashley." Ethan's voice was low, warm, calm. "Look at me. At me. In my eyes."

It was the last place she wanted to focus, but her eyes were drawn to his. As soon as her gaze met his, everything in her stilled. It was the last place she should find safety, but her heart knew him and refused to feel anything else.

"You're okay. You're safe. No matter what happens, I am right here beside you. I will protect you." Those last words hammered with emphasis, slow and heavy.

She couldn't look him in the eye anymore.

Ashley leaned back from his grasp and exhaled, panic floating away with his promises. She had no idea how he'd done it, but she hoped he didn't have to again. The way her pulse pounded now had absolutely nothing to do with fear.

This was probably worse.

As much as she knew close proximity to Ethan was dangerous to her heart and as much as she wanted to walk away to protect herself, she couldn't. Sean's life—her life—depended on their teaming up.

And, boy, when they were all safe, was Sean going

to hear from her about this entire setup, from painting a bull's-eye on her back to making her work with Ethan Kincaid again.

For now, there was work to do. Authority to assert. "You have to take me to my car."

Ethan's head came up, eyebrows high in confusion. "Your car? At the airport?" He shook his head. "No way. For all we know, there are people staking it out."

Control. What she needed right now was control, and she was about to take it. She needed to be in charge if she wanted to survive this. She needed to fool herself into believing something was in her power. "Doubtful. They saw you come in all John Wayne and take me out of there like your truck was on fire. They're long gone from the airport, focused on my apartment or somewhere else." She pulled her seat belt across and latched it with a definite click. "We're going to the airport."

"There is no way I'm—"

"The keys to the post-office box are in it. The box is up north, in Black River. I go up every couple of weeks to check on my grandparents' cabin and to get his mail." That was something she should have seen before. The fact Sean had rented a postbox an hour away instead of a more convenient location in Syracuse. He was trying to protect her even while he used her. Maybe she should be grateful, and she would be, after she tore him apart for doing this to her in the first place. "We have to get those keys or we can't get into the box. There's no other way."

There it was. The twitch in his right temple. It popped up when he couldn't say what was on his mind. What she wouldn't give to know what he was thinking right about now. Or not, because it probably wasn't butterflies and rainbows.

"This is the single dumbest thing I've ever done."

Ethan pulled out his cell phone and punched the screen so hard it was a wonder cracks didn't form. "I have to let Mitch know we've changed plans and we'll be late getting you to the safe house." He held the phone tight, muttering. "It'll be by the grace of God if you don't get us both killed."

God. Since when did He worry about Ashley?

And since when did Ethan worry about God?

FIVE

The clouds had moved out and the sky above the Syracuse airport was blacker than Ethan could ever remember seeing it. It seemed even the stars were hiding from the menace Ethan and Ashley faced.

As they turned onto the road to the airport, Ethan's head ached. The drive had been short, but each passing moment increased the tension in his muscles until the pressure pounded behind his right eyeball. He'd never endured a migraine. This had better not be the first time.

He'd been in a lot of rough situations in the past, seen a buddy die just inches away from him, thought a time or two the movie of his own life was about to play out in front of his eyes. But never, ever had the stakes been as high as they were right now. There was no telling where Sean was or what kind of danger he was in. Danger Ethan had knowingly encouraged him to confront.

As much as he wanted to pretend this was all about getting to the bottom of this investigation and rescuing Sean, it was only a small part of this mission. The life in the seat next to him meant so much more than he cared to admit. He'd already seen it nearly snuffed out once, on his watch. It had taken God to help him overcome the guilt, and the scar still seared. If something happened to Ashley again, even God couldn't help him forgive himself.

"You're way too quiet." Ashley's voice cut through the darkness.

He could say the same of her. For the entire drive, he'd been aware of her fragile hold on herself. Her words were too measured. The forced rhythm spoke of carefully practiced control.

How long would she be able to hold it together? In the parking lot, instinct had driven him to force her to meet his eyes. A mistake if he'd ever made one. Even in the midst of her losing control of every part of herself, he'd been aware of her as if five years hadn't passed. Aware of the way she still smelled faintly like summer, even in the early chill of a New York spring. Aware of the way her cheek felt warm and smooth against his palm. Aware of the way he had never gotten over the desire to pull her close and shield her from the world, pull her near and kiss her in a way that made her forget everything but him.

There was no chance of that ever happening, not after what he'd seen when she was in the hospital. He'd gone to tell her how he felt but stopped outside the door when he'd seen Sean there, holding her hand, coaxing her first smile since the incident.

Ethan had conceded. He'd made the conscious, soul-shattering decision to leave her with the better man, the one who wasn't stealing her dream, the one who'd shared a lifetime with her already.

He sure couldn't say that out loud. "I'm trying to figure out how we're going to pull this off without getting us killed. This is foolish."

"But necessary if you want Sean's intel." She sighed. "Look, I parked right up near the gate. You don't even have to pull in and risk being seen. You can watch me get the keys out of the car, and I'll come right back to your truck. I can't pull out and run without passing right by you. We can go wherever we have to go until the post office opens, I'll get Sean's data and we'll go from there." She edged around so he could see her face. "I promise."

Ethan bit the inside of his cheek and looked away from those green eyes he'd missed an awful lot over the past five years. Ashley was one of those people who never broke a promise. "I don't like this. Give me your keys and let me go." She was being as stubborn today as the day he'd let her question his authority and had taken a bullet for his letting her do it.

"If anyone is watching, we'll be gone before they can make a move." She ignored him and pointed as they drove past the lot. "Look. I'm the little silver crossover right there. You can't lose me."

Ethan edged closer to the gate at the entrance to the lot. He scanned the area, lit by a large streetlight. No shadows moved. The nearest car to hers in the near-empty corner was six spaces away. "Against my better judgment."

"But you have to have those thumb drives." She grinned, obviously delighted to have her way. "I always loved getting you over a barrel."

"No kidding."

She pushed the door open and looked at him, her eyes serious. "Whatever's going on is bad, isn't it?"

Worse than she thought, but the fear etching a line in her forehead kept him from saying so. "It's going to be okay." If Sean wasn't dead already. If those drives were still at the post office. If a thousand other things went exactly right.

Ashley crossed the space and slipped into her car, tossing him a grim wave as she leaned toward the glove box.

Just a minute more and they'd be on the road again.

His taut muscles eased but tightened again at the sound of screeching tires. A flash of headlights and a large SUV appeared, cutting across the empty space, bumper guard slamming into Ashley's small vehicle at the end of the row and driving it sideways in a flurry of glass and metal.

The world jolted in a metal-twisting crash. Ashley's head whipped and smacked into the exploding pillow of the side air bag as the car rocked dangerously, threatening to tip. Another screech and her car rocked again, harder this time, sliding sideways. Ashley tasted blood as the world rocketed with stars.

Then silence. Distant shouts. Nothing came into focus except cold air on her face and the glimmer of glass in her lap. Glass. In her lap. Why was there glass in her lap? She tried to lift her hand to brush it off, but her wrist was stuck, trapped between the console and her body, which felt too heavy to move, like an elephant had chosen her as its resting place for the night.

There was a sound behind her. A click. Familiar.

Ethan.

Ethan had seen what happened and was coming to get her. Like the last time. He'd save her. Her mind landed on the soft swish of a gate lifting. She wanted to call to him for help, to tell him she was alive, but her brain wouldn't tell her lips to form the words.

There were other words outside of her, ones she didn't understand, then footsteps, louder than anything else, and more distant shouts. A hand appeared, sweeping the depleted air bag from the window. A face. Dark. Lined. Angry. "Where is Turner's information?" The accent was heavy, almost too hard to decipher.

It was too foggy, muddy, cloudy. Sean? He was in Afghanistan. She tried to move. Her arm was trapped. "I—"

The word was jammed up her mouth. Why couldn't she say something?

The man reached in and pinched her jaw between his thumb and fingers. A low cry strangled in her throat. Her whole world centered on the pain as he yanked her head to face him, so much less gentler than Ethan a half hour earlier. "I will ask you again. Where are the drives from your friend Sean Turner?"

Scan? With a sudden rush, clarity returned. The phone call. The man trying to take her. "No." Ashley tried to jerk away from the hand that grasped her, but the man tightened his hold, shooting pain through her neck and into her spine.

The passenger door wrenched open and a second man climbed in, flooding relief through her. She was saved.

Then he spoke, the same voice from her apartment. "Just take her with you, like we planned. Worry about the drives later. If we have her there's no one to decode the information and we can use her to ensure Turner will talk." He shoved her body to the side and yanked her arm free, sending a bolt of pain through her. Seizing her under the shoulder, he pulled Ashley toward him, driving her side into the console. He was taking her.

Where was Ethan? Surely he was close and she hadn't dreamed everything about this horrid night. He wouldn't let them get away.

She tried to scream but her lungs hurt too much. She wanted to fight but stars popped in her vision as pain ripped into her side and the world faded into silent darkness.

Ethan was out of his truck and running before the SUV backed up and hit Ashley's car a second time. The sound of grinding metal crawled down his spine in an effort to throw him to the ground. He pushed on. If Ashley died, it would be his fault. He never should have let her go alone, just as he never should have let her circle that house alone. This was why Mitchum had said he should step away from the case. His emotional attachment to Ashley dulled the edge from his training.

His boots thudded on the pavement as he assessed the situation. Security was lighter at night, dampening the speed of response. Even if they'd instantly seen what happened, it would take time for help to make it across the parking lot.

It was just Ethan and the two men who converged on Ashley's vehicle, rear passenger side crushed like an aluminum can.

The men didn't seem to have weapons, but Ethan was too far away. There was nothing he could do either way. He needed to move, to save her.

It seemed to take days to reach her vehicle, where one man leaned in the front window. Ethan dealt with him first. Without breaking stride, he ducked low, his shoulder catching the man in the stomach. They tumbled to the ground, the man's head striking the light pole Ashley's crossover rested against, a strangled scream echoing off the nearby parking garage.

Ethan rolled, rose on one knee and balanced himself as he shook off the blow, prepared for the coming attack.

There was a muffled curse from Ashley's car then sirens in the distance. Another curse and the second man appeared around the rear of the vehicle. He leveled a gaze on Ethan and prepared to launch, but a distant shout jerked his attention behind him. With a dark stare, he threatened Ethan without words, then, uttering something incomprehensible, leaped for his damaged SUV, his partner following. The pair roared off backward down the aisle before

Ethan could react. Still, the chill of that stare burned an image in his eyes that he knew he'd see in his sleep for many nights to come.

He needed to call Mitchum, to put local law enforcement on the alert, but first… First he needed to know Ashley was still alive.

Ethan pushed himself up and shook out his shoulder, leaning into the car as Ashley groaned and lolled her head to face him. Her eyes fluttered, and she pulled in a gasp, trying to back away from him.

He laid a hand on her shoulder, comforting her for the second time in less than half an hour. "Ash, it's me. Ethan. You're safe." *For now.*

Her head jerked and she closed her eyes then opened them again, blinking against hair tangled in her lashes.

Ethan pushed the light blond strands away, afraid to move her.

"So much for not getting anyone else involved." Her voice was barely more than a whisper as sirens drew nearer.

Ethan's muscles threatened to drop him to the ground, relief relaxing the tension as he pulled his hand away. If she was going to default to sarcasm, she was going to be fine. "True. But we'll be okay." He hoped, though he wasn't about to make a promise he wasn't sure could be kept. He'd tried to keep local law enforcement out of this for fear of blowing their investigation, but there was no way to run with Ashley injured. He'd keep his mouth shut and let them make their own assumptions.

An EMT stuck his head in the passenger-door opening, destroying any further words. "What do we have here?"

Ethan let himself be pushed to the side as more workers arrived on the scene, shouting orders and asking questions. His muscles refused to fight, the images too familiar. Lights, sirens, emergency personnel converging on Ashley, working to save her from his lapse in judgment.

Again.

SIX

"All in all, if you're a praying woman, you should be thanking God for those side air bags. You'd have cracked your skull without them."

The nurse, Tricia, made a note in the computer she'd wheeled into the room. "Not many people could walk away from that kind of impact without side bags. Here's hoping they find that driver. Hit-and-runners are cowards. Probably saw an opportunity to turn doughnuts in the parking lot and it all went south from there." She clicked the button on the mouse, her bright red hair bouncing on the shoulders of her purple scrubs. "You'll likely be released in the next couple of hours."

Ashley eased her head to look out the window. The sky hung close and inky. She barely remembered the ambulance ride to the hospital, where Ethan told the staff she was under police protection and needed a private room. Next thing she knew, he'd vanished.

She wrinkled her nose and focused on the intense black of the night. Dawn must be soon if the adage was true. The past few hours had been so disjointed, she had no idea what time it was. Surely this couldn't be the same night she'd stepped off the plane from Albany.

And Nurse Tricia had the nerve to tell her she ought to be thanking God.

Thank God? For what?

Now that she had time alone without Ethan to muddle her thoughts, she'd discovered a whole lot more questions than answers. They were answers she couldn't get immediately. Ethan hadn't made an appearance since she'd been wheeled into the emergency room, though she'd caught a glimpse of Mitchum outside her door. He'd tried to get in earlier, but the nurses had told him to wait, buying Ashley some precious quiet.

Ethan and Sean both had some explaining to do. There was more to this than Ethan had told her.

She fought a shudder, refusing to be afraid. Sure, she was safe now, but those men would return. And maybe next time Ethan wouldn't be there to stop them, just as he hadn't been there the very first time.

Ashley let her thoughts wander to a memory she normally had the strength to keep locked away.

That evening, she had watched his patrol car glide up and let him step out before she touched the door handle, giving herself a chance to adjust to the sight of him. It always jolted her, the way he looked in his uniform. Taller, broader of shoulder, sandy hair just starting to curl on the ends under his patrol cap. The uniform made him look menacing…if you were a criminal. Totally heart-melting if you were the girl in love with him.

Especially if you couldn't let him know. They worked together. And he was friends with Sean…who'd pulled out a ring at what was supposed to be a friendly dinner last night. What had he been thinking? Deployment had gotten to him, had him looking for stability. She couldn't tell him where her feelings really rested. She could just go on pretending they were all friends.

Reeling in her thoughts, Ashley ground her cap onto her head and stepped out of the patrol car to meet Ethan at the rear bumper.

He tugged at the end of his sleeve, eyes focused on the front of the house. It was silent, save the whisper of wind in the trees. "Think it's a false alarm?"

"It would be nice, but this guy's already got one pending assault charge and has been threatened with demotion."

Ashley pulled her attention to the front of the house. It looked no different from any other military duplex on the street. Beige vinyl siding broken up by windows, the blinds tightly closed. Cement steps leading up to a white front door. "Looks empty."

"Neighbor said he heard screams." Ethan stepped in front of her. "Well, let's hope for the best. We can make sure all is well then grab a burger." He stepped around a small puddle. "You can tell me what's going on with you and Sean."

The toe of Ashley's boot scuffed the sidewalk. Why did he bring Sean up? After the humiliation the two of them had endured last night—humiliation Ethan never needed to know about—Ashley would be happy to let things lie until she could hash them out with Sean and maybe, just maybe, leave their friendship intact.

Ethan didn't seem to notice her misstep. She stepped behind him onto the cement porch and waited for him to take the lead as ranking officer.

Balling his fist, Ethan pounded on the door, his voice dropping an octave, quivering Ashley's stomach in a way that was definitely not professional. "Military police."

Silence.

The kind of silence that made the hairs on the back of Ashley's neck stand at attention.

Ethan felt it, too. He glanced at her, raised an eyebrow and pounded on the door again, right hand resting near his weapon.

Ashley squinted, her gut knowing this was all wrong. "I'll check the back."

"I'll do it. If this goes bad, it's going to get dangerous."

"I said I'd check the back." She didn't know why she stood up to him, just knew the thing with Sean left her needing to exert control.

Ethan's jaw stiffened with the challenge. "I said I'd take the back, *Corporal*. It's his likely escape route. Give me time to get into position then knock again. Maybe it will flush him out. Just be ready to back me up."

Man, how she hated it when he treated her like a girl who needed protection. Ashley wanted to argue, but training kept her mouth shut as she backed down to the grass and let him step past her.

He didn't even look at her.

Not that she blamed him. She'd bucked his rank. As much as she dreaded it, they might not be able to work together anymore, not with her personal feelings twisting her in knots.

Stepping up to the porch, Ashley let her fingers rest on her pistol. It wasn't that she needed the weapon, but it boosted her confidence to know it was at the ready. It was her security blanket, her best friend on the job. One she hoped she never needed.

From the back of the house, violating their plan, Ethan pounded and called out.

What was he doing?

There was an explosion of motion. A man charged from the house, throwing the screen door open hard enough to knock Ashley to the ground. Scrambling to her feet, Ashley drew her weapon and leveled it at the man on the porch above her.

He froze, eyeing Ashley wildly.

The anger in his expression chilled her blood. *Lord Jesus, let this end well. Protect us all.*

Ashley's weapon aimed steadily as he slowly lifted his hands. Where there should be fear, unwavering peace settled. She'd played out this scenario more times than she could count, and she trusted Ethan was coming around the corner. In seconds this would be over.

Except…the man dived from the porch, driving her into the cement stoop of the other duplex. Pain exploded from her lower spine, shooting stars across her view of the man's face, contorted in anger. He gripped her wrist and struggled for her weapon, squeezing so tightly her bones felt like brittle twigs. She called for Ethan as her attacker dragged her hand lower.

The roar seemed to come simultaneously from inside and outside of her body. A burning in her side defied anything she'd felt before. A surge of adrenaline made her skin tingle and her ears ring as the man backed away. Her hands fell to her sides, weapon dropping to the ground as her eyes went to her stomach. Red spread against the camouflage, blurring the pattern.

Ashley sank to her knees as the world returned in a rush. Shouts. Running feet. Ethan's voice. "Officer down!" There was a jagged edge to the words as the calm confidence he always wore broke.

And then he was kneeling in front of her. The edges of the world narrowed to his face, where unfamiliar fear sparked in his eyes, a gash open at the side of his brow. He shook her shoulders. "Ash! Breathe!"

Breathe? Her lungs burned. Her stomach flamed.

Breathe? Her head lolled to one side, too heavy for her neck to support.

Ethan's fingers dug into her shoulders. "You have to breathe!"

With a cry, Ashley sucked air into her lungs, oxygen firing pulses to her brain that let pain and reality barge in. Her hands grasped her stomach. She was going to die. "Ethan…" The word slurred, didn't sound like a word at all, maybe hadn't even made it out of her mouth.

"I've got you. Help's coming." He slipped a hand behind her head and lowered her to the ground.

It felt too much like death. She needed to stay upright. Needed to stay alive. She tried to shake her head but it wouldn't move. She lifted her hand and grasped the rough fabric of his uniform at his chest, pulse pounding black behind her eyes. "No." Her eyes followed her hand, took in her fingers coated in red, Ethan's chest covered in streaks. Blood. Her blood.

Her ears rang. Her body pounded. And darkness she could no longer fight shuttered the world—

"Ms. Colson?" Nurse Tricia's voice broke through the memory.

Cold sweat slicked Ashley's skin.

Abandoning her computer, the nurse moved closer. "You look distressed. How's your pain?"

Unfathomable. Untouchable. But that wasn't the pain the nurse was asking about. There was nothing to fix that.

Ashley ran her hands along the bed rail and re-centered herself in the room. "Not too bad right now."

Skepticism wrinkled Nurse Tricia's forehead, but she turned to type in a note. Probably about Ashley lying. "Well, I'm pretty sure what's waiting outside will help." With a wink, she wheeled the cart out of the room, tossing a "You can go in now" over her shoulder as she took a left up the hallway.

So Ethan had reappeared? Ashley sat straighter and swept her hand through her hair, unable to decide if she wanted to hide or beg him to hold her close.

Special Agent Craig Mitchum peeked around the door, dragging disappointment with him. "Mind if I step in?" His blond hair stood on end as though he'd raked his hand through it more than once. He glanced up the hallway and back at Ashley, hesitant to enter the room.

Ashley swallowed her disappointment. "Might as well."

She could tell him no, but he'd haunt the hallway, pacing and amping up her tension. At least this way she could offer him a seat. She didn't even want to think about why he was standing guard.

No, she couldn't dwell on that right now. Here, at least temporarily, there was safety. She waved to the chair near the foot of the bed.

Mitchum settled into the seat, but he didn't relax. "How are you feeling?"

"A little stiff, but my guess is tomorrow is going to be a whole other story. Any word on the guys who hit me?" *And tried to take me?* Twice. Twice in one night someone had tried to harm her.

The heart monitor pinged faster. How many times would they try before they succeeded?

"You okay?" Mitchum watched the monitor's rise and fall. "Want me to call the nurse?"

Ashley willed those telltale beats to slow. "I'm fine. Any word?"

Mitchum eyed her for a moment as though he knew she was lying, then sat back. "Local law enforcement found the SUV a couple of miles from the airport." He returned his gaze to Ashley. "And if anyone asks, you were the victim of a random attack."

Ethan had already briefed her just before the police talked to her in the ER.

"Where's Ethan?" She needed his solid presence, his reassuring words. Outside the window, the darkness began to give way to faint day, yet he hadn't appeared.

"Kincaid? Last I saw he was downstairs getting coffee." Mitchum glanced at the door, then sat forward, elbows resting on his knees. "What on earth possessed Kincaid to take you to the airport?"

"What?"

"Stupid, rookie move." Mitchum shook his head. "First he ditches me, insists you have to go with him... You don't separate from your partner, and you don't return to the scene where your asset was almost abducted." Mitchum clasped his hands. "Something's going on with him. Something not like him."

Oh, no. He was totally acting like himself. Switching up the plan on his partner at a crucial time, disappearing...

Still, she couldn't let Ethan shoulder the blame. "I made him take me."

"Why? I'm assuming you retrieved the intel Turner sent?" If he leaned any farther forward in the chair, he'd slide right onto the floor. "Who has it?"

"We don't have anything." She didn't know Ethan's partner well enough to trust him with everything. Let Ethan decide when it was the right time to talk.

Her back twinged between her shoulder blades and she shifted, adjusting the pillows. "I needed the key to Sean's box to get the package, and it was in my car."

"You passed the key to Kincaid?"

She had, just before the ambulance doors shut between them.

Mitchum shook his head and smiled. "Turner…he's a smart guy."

"You've met him?"

"Never known the pleasure, but I've heard about him. Guy's a computer genius. Our unit's trying to recruit him. It's no wonder they sent him on this mission instead of me. I'd have never been able to dig up half of what it's being reported he's sent back."

The heart monitor ticked up again. Ethan's unit was recruiting Sean? And Ethan? He hadn't spoken a word of it.

SEVEN

Ethan pressed the elevator button, then leaned his forehead against the wall. His gut needed to settle down, and the bitter smell of the coffee he'd grabbed for Mitchum wasn't helping. Hospitals and coffee were deadly combinations. The last time he'd drunk a cup of the brew had been in the waiting room while Ashley was in surgery, and the smell still curled his stomach.

The short ride up moved much too slowly for Ethan's taste, crawling to the third floor inch by precious inch. He stared at the doors, coffee hot in his hand, grateful to have Mitchum. He'd needed a few minutes to pace the lobby, formulate a plan, think through what to do next.

The whole time, all he'd wanted was to race upstairs and see for himself she was in one piece, to pull her close and tell her he was sorry. But with his emotions so high, he knew better. His mouth would spout all of his feelings, betraying Sean and leaving Ashley in the awkward position of putting him back in his place on the outskirts of her life. The life he still had to protect. If he wanted to keep her safe, he had to block his feelings, keep her at a distance so his mind could stay in the game until the end.

Local law enforcement believed Ashley's attack was a late-night hit-and-run by a couple of drunk drivers. The

SUV had been found behind a shopping center a few miles from the airport, and when they'd contacted the owner, he hadn't realized the vehicle was missing. Ethan was certain they'd find only the owner's prints inside. These criminals knew what they were doing.

The next step was to get Ashley to the safe house and have Mitchum pick up Sean's thumb drives. Even though Ethan itched to call up his chain of command to ask for help, he knew better. With someone clearly listening in, this mission required stealth. If the bad guys caught wind the endgame was near, they'd kill Sean and run. He was only an asset to them until the knowledge in his head was compromised. With Ashley's software and Sean's intel in their possession, they could bring down these guys and get Sean home.

Then what? Ethan would go to his next case and Ashley would return to her life.

To her solitary fear.

In the time he'd been surveilling her, he'd seen it. Ashley kept to herself. She didn't go out for coffee. Didn't have visitors. All she did was work.

Ethan dropped his head back against the wall of the elevator. She didn't even go to church anymore, at least not that he'd seen.

He wasn't ready to let her return to that life. There was no way to miss the way she looked at him, with a skittishness that said she expected him to run in the opposite direction at any second. This, her panic, was more than fear of facing a gun… It was fear of being alone when she was vulnerable.

The elevator door swished open, but Ethan didn't move. That fear… He'd caused it. Five years ago he'd bolted from her life half because he didn't want her to know he'd attained her dream and half because he couldn't stay, loving her when he knew his best friend was in love with her, too. If Ethan had stayed, his feelings would have been exposed and it would have been the end of a friendship. Two men fighting for the love of one woman who deserved better than him.

Sean had been the one to stick by Ashley's side when she was broken. Not Ethan. Sean was the man who deserved her. The one who, despite their broken engagement, still held court in her life. Not the man whose major life commitment was to the army. The man who'd failed to protect his partner in the clinch the day Ashley was shot.

The door started to slide shut again. Ethan hefted himself up and stepped out, half tempted to put his fist through a wall. He'd wanted to confront the danger, but he'd read the situation wrong. And then he'd thwarted their plan when he'd heard noise inside and banged on the door, spooking the gunman straight toward Ashley. If he'd done anything differently, Ashley would have the life she deserved today.

Young and stupid. Time, grief and experience had matured him, and he knew a mission such as this required his feelings to be firmly locked away.

Mitchum pushed off of the wall and pocketed his phone as Ethan approached. "Tell me you brought coffee."

Ethan offered a halfhearted grin. Black sludge had to run through his partner's veins. "I can find you an IV. Open a line and fix you right up." He held out the cup. "How's Ashley?"

"Resting."

Ethan nodded. He'd wait to go in. Maybe she'd get some sleep before the doc released her and they needed to move. Too long in one place was dangerous. "Any other word?"

Mitchum clicked his teeth and stared into his coffee cup.

Ethan recognized the move. Bad news was headed their way. "What?"

"When was the last time you called Colonel Franklin?"

"When we got the message from Turner. Why?"

"The safe house was compromised."

Ethan fought the urge to slump against the wall. They had only one safe house in the Syracuse area. "What happened?"

"Neighbor called the cops about an hour ago. Someone busted in the kitchen door, made a mess of the place. The only people who officially knew we were taking Ashley there were me, you and the colonel."

"And I'm not the one passing off information." Ethan curled his fist. This should have been easy. Collect Ashley, collect the evidence and lie low in the safe house.

"It's not me, either. And we know it's not the colonel. If it is, we might as well give up."

"We have to assume someone was able to hear the phone conversation." Ethan pulled his phone from his pocket. It was as dumb a phone as the government could buy, one in use strictly for this mission. There was no GPS, no Wi-Fi. "Either my phone or headquarters has a bug."

"And you can't call the colonel and tell him, or you risk tipping our hand. If it's one of our people, any code words have already been compromised. I got the message because it wouldn't be news to the bad guys." Mitchum dragged his thumb around the lid of the cup. "The safe house could have been a random break-in, but I don't think we should take the chance."

Neither did Ethan. Ashley's life was too valuable.

"You've got that look on your face." Mitchum sipped his coffee and eyed Ethan over the top of the cup.

"What look?"

"How well did you know this girl before? You won't trust her with anybody else, won't let go of this investigation…and every time she comes up, you get all moony-eyed."

Ethan schooled his expression. "Moony-eyed? You been talking to my great-grandmother, Mitch? Don't confuse deep thought with deep emotions. And don't suggest again that I need to be off of this case. I'm the one who convinced Turner to get involved. It's my responsibility to get him out of this, and both of us know she's the only way."

He needed to walk away before he said too much, and the one place to go was Ashley's room. Without another word, he twisted the doorknob and stepped inside, expecting to find her asleep. Instead her laser gaze should have melted him on the spot. "You're awake."

She sniffed, eyes hard. "And you're a liar."

The words hit with the force of fists, the pain so physical he couldn't even ask what she meant.

"Tell me the truth, Ethan. For the first time since…" Ashley waved a hand that seemed to encompass all eternity.

He found his voice, shut the door and took a step closer. "What truth?" The question was guarded, because there was some truth he could never tell.

"The truth about Sean. About why he's in Afghanistan."

The tone of the words said everything rode on his answer, an answer he suspected she already knew. Mitch was the only one who could have told her.

Not for the first time, Ethan wanted to have serious words with his partner. What was he thinking? If anyone had told her, it should have been Ethan…or Sean himself.

"What do you want to know?"

Ashley's face was hard, the kind of expression she'd worn on duty when confronting drunk drivers like the ones who'd killed her parents. It was the kind of expression that bordered on hatred. It was one he'd never thought he'd see aimed at him. The chill raised the hair on his arms.

"When did he start talking to Intelligence? And why didn't he tell me?" She eased up until her posture was ramrod-straight. "Why didn't *you* tell me? You lied about why he's in Afghanistan, said he was doing you a favor."

He hadn't lied. He just hadn't told her the whole truth. In this moment, that explanation wasn't going to fly very far. "I told you the truth earlier. He's not with Intelligence." Not officially anyway.

"I want my questions answered." Every angle of her face was tighter than he'd seen since the shooting. She was in pain, but it was impossible to tell if the pain was physical or emotional…or a volatile combination.

The set of her jaw said even more. Control. As long as she was interrogating Ethan, there was no room for fear. Control had been her companion all night, her coping mechanism. If it was that important to her, he'd let her have it for the few moments he could.

Pocketing his phone, Ethan sank to the chair at the foot of the bed. If he stood close to her, he'd risk touching her. "Fire away. I owe you that much."

The look on her face said he owed her a whole lot more. "I know how Intelligence works. I studied it before…" There it was. That flash of regret, maybe even anger. "There are other units to call, units that get the information you uncover and use it. Level after level of people involved. You and your partner act like lone wolves without a pack leader."

Go figure she'd lead with the hard stuff. It was the one question Ethan wished he could ignore because once Ashley figured out she was more qualified to do his job than he was, she'd either hate him forever or descend into a funk that God alone could get her out of, and it didn't seem as though she was on speaking terms with Him.

"You're not answering."

"Okay." Ethan sat forward in his chair, but the weight of what he was about to say dragged his shoulders into a slump. "I did go to Intelligence, then into Special Operations. A couple of years ago there was a series of cyber attacks on our government infrastructure, and it made some big brass push for implementation of a program to protect ourselves against cyber terrorism. Prior to that, it was on the radar but not in the center of the screen."

"I remember." Ashley's expression turned thoughtful. "I was about to go under, but something about the government being hacked made more people look at their localized security. That attack is what made my company viable and let me leave my day job to focus on Colson Solutions full-time."

"Well, something good came of it." Though the military would never think so. "There was a lot more to it than the public learned, even more than I can tell you. The attacks weren't merely computer-based. We came close to some nasty events within our borders. Some resources were shifted for crimes like the one we're dealing with now—cyber criminals who do more than hack machines, but who go physically active, as well. Terror networks that hack in to destroy the network and the people who run it and also siphon funds to bankroll themselves. We're still tracking down those initial hackers and the groups behind them."

Ashley nodded. "They use stolen data to gain cash and intel for real-world use, requiring brains and brawn to bring them down?"

"If you want to word it that way."

Was it good or bad that Ashley had shifted from angry frustration to cold knowing? At least she wasn't about to throw a punch. "Joint Special Operations Command formed a Special Mission Unit made up of a handful of elite teams, pairing agents who could provide both mind and muscle. We work off the radar, without anyone else knowing. We don't even have a name, no unit crest, no written chain of command. On paper, we're Intelligence, but in reality we're not. When you're talking about hackers, nothing is secure, not the phones, not the internet, nothing. Things are done very low-tech with old-school technology such as secure landlines, coded snail mail, even handwritten messages passed from one person to another. All unhackable. Unfortunately that hasn't stopped someone on the inside from handing out information they shouldn't be dispersing."

"You're a part of that unit."

Ethan nodded slowly, coming to the part he dreaded most. "Although the time line was pushed up, this has been in the works since before we all joined the army. Your recruiter probably talked up your test scores, your computer interests. You didn't start out wanting to go into Intelligence, but it was talked up to you before you signed up, all through Basic and Military Police School. Before you got out of Basic, you were tapped to take classes and tests…all computer-based. Sean was. I was. They were looking for the soldiers who could drive these teams."

Ashley's expression didn't change. Just her eyes. That unbearable sadness he'd seen before when they'd talked about what could have been her future in the military.

He couldn't stop now. She needed to know everything or she wouldn't trust him, especially if Mitch kept dropping bread crumbs. "You know, Sean and you… When it came to computers, you were naturals, and you fed off each other. Probably because you grew up together and had that history. I'm good, but you have way more talent than me."

Hardness edged into Ashley's expression. This time, though, there was a tinge of something like jealousy. "So you referred Sean for this SMU. But when? He's never showed an interest in being anything other than an infantryman."

"Don't fool yourself. Look at the program you wrote. Like most guys, Sean likes the excitement of infantry, but you know where his real love is." Sitting back in the chair, Ethan tried to project nonchalance. Maybe, if he acted as though this was no big deal, she'd take that vibe and run with it.

"When the unit was fast-tracked, I was already in Special Forces, already making a name for myself with computers." He shed the nonchalance and pressed his fists into his thighs. She wouldn't go for it anyway. "Sean had an inkling about where I was working, but no confirmation. When he uncovered this breach, he contacted me. When we needed him, he agreed to do the job.

"He's more than a Field Ordering Officer gathering intel. He's been actively digging, gathering intelligence on who comes and goes from the FOB and a couple of the combat outposts, listening in on radio chatter and phone calls, downloading emails… He's been gathering all of the information he can to take down these guys. There's no telling what's on those drives, but it's likely enough to expose the ringleaders and end their operation."

Ashley's nose twitched, betraying the storm underneath her calm exterior. "You're telling me Sean's actively involved in this unit and has lied to me for…how long?" The hurt in her posture testified to her feelings for Sean.

"To protect you."

"I'm not a child who needs to be protected." She balled the white sheet in her fists. "I nearly died. My weakness cost me everything and now I find out the dream was bigger than I thought it could be. There's not much more to protect me from, is there?"

Something in Ethan's chest tightened. If he wasn't careful, he'd end up in a room right beside her.

Ethan hefted himself out of the chair and knelt by her hand on the bed. "You wanted Intelligence more than anything. You held it in your hands and had to watch it go away. How could I stand in front of you and know I got what was rightfully yours?

"There's no person who could do this job like you could. You'd be brilliant, the best out there. It's not lost on me that what I'm telling you hurts. We talked about this very thing more than once—the need for a unit like this. It's tough to swallow that your vision came to reality without you. Trust me. I know."

He'd watched it play out in Sean's relationship with her. Even now, he could see them in his mind's eye huddled together over this program they'd developed, the one that was the key to saving Sean's life now. "Sean wouldn't have involved you, but he was backed into a corner when it came to this cipher business. With a mole in the unit, he couldn't risk passing along a typical decryption key.

So he created something that lies in your head. Even I don't know what it is. He did it because you're good at this, because he knew you could pick up the pieces if it all fell apart."

When he reached for her, she jerked her hand away, laying her arm across her stomach. "Tell me the rest."

"Okay. But you're not going to like it."

"I already don't like it. I've been lied to, almost kidnapped, and made a target for terrorists because I'm the only person on the planet who's a threat to them. And now I'm laid up in the hospital when Sean needs me."

Not for more than another hour if Ethan had anything to do with it. He couldn't risk keeping her in one spot any longer, no matter what the doctors said. Since Mitchum had dropped the bomb about the safe house, Ethan needed to come up with someplace secure. There was one option, but it had never been fully vetted as a safe house and conditions needed to be 100 percent perfect. Not likely at this time of year.

He couldn't lay that plan out until he gave Ashley everything. "I told you earlier I'd lay all of my cards on the table. Well… There are three of us on a team, typically one undercover and two supporting."

"Who's your third man?" From the look in Ashley's eyes, she thought it was Sean, though they'd worked together only from a distance. No, the truth was worse, at least for Sean.

"When I joined up, I was partnered with Sergeant Jacob Reynolds. We were together for two years." The words tasted like bile. "Sean tipped us off to this scheme, and Reynolds went in to investigate. I told you our last man in-country was unsuccessful. It was Reynolds, and as the only person we could trust, the only person who already knew what was happening, Sean's his replacement." He reached for her hand and she didn't pull away. "Like Sean, Reynolds was abducted by insurgents. We found his body five weeks later."

EIGHT

Ashley couldn't get oxygen into her lungs fast enough.

She breathed in through her nose, out through her mouth. *Regulate. Regulate. Regulate.* No way had her best friend done all of this behind her back. No way had he stepped into a job this dangerous without telling her or linked up with the man Ashley had once thought she might love. The world wasn't that surreal.

"Ashley…" Ethan's voice cut through the fog, but it did nothing to soothe her.

Everything was upside down. She was the key to rescuing Sean, whose life was in a more tenuous balance than she'd realized. And Ethan…

Before the thought could gel, the door to her room flew open and Mitchum's linebacker shoulders filled the space. "Kincaid. Outside."

All motion in Ashley stopped. Something was very wrong.

Ethan stood, looked down at Ashley and then shot a warning to his partner. "Now's not a good—"

"Now." Mitchum's voice brooked no argument.

Ethan looked at her again and Ashley flicked her hand toward the door. Let him walk out the door and never return. As soon as he dealt with whatever his partner wanted, she was going to tell him she wanted someone else—anyone else—involved, even if it violated every protocol of his little secret operation. His presence brought up too much emotion for her to handle.

When she laid hands on Sean again, he was going to wish…

As the door closed behind Ethan, nausea roiled in her stomach. Sean was missing, the result of the secret he'd kept from her. There may never be a chance to confront him about the story he'd left untold.

Lies shriveled under the weight of realization. Sean needed her. Ethan needed her. Sean had encoded data in one way and, even with the decryption software in Ethan's hands, she was the only one who could decipher it and get him out of this alive.

Her only choice if she wanted to find her best friend and save her own life was to trust the last man she wanted to trust. The last man who deserved her trust.

The door flung open and Ethan marched in, his face tight, white lines dragging down between his eyebrows. He flung a duffel bag on the bed by her feet and tossed a baseball cap beside it. "Get dressed. We have to go."

"Go where?" Ashley sat up, grasping the thin blanket so tight her hands nearly turned the same color as the bleached sheets. "Ethan?"

"Mitchum and I have been taking turns monitoring security feeds. There was a guy asking questions at the front desk. He skirted security and is going floor to floor. He started in the ER. He's bound to be looking for you."

Ashley grasped the clothes Ethan pulled from the bag and stared at them as though they were foreign objects.

"Put them on. They belong to one of the nurses. She was planning to go to the gym when she got off shift in the morning, but thought she'd give them up to the cause.

She's about your size." Ethan glanced at the door. "We spotted one guy on camera, but surely there are more." He tossed her a sad smirk and disappeared into the hall, calling over his shoulder, "You've got thirty seconds."

The click of the door galvanized Ashley's muscles. She slipped from the bed, adrenaline dulling the pain in her body, and changed as fast as she could. The shoes were a hair too tight, but cramped toes were the least of her worries.

Snatching the cap from the end of the bed, Ashley paused. The Yankees. At any other time, the Red Sox fan in her would have revolted at the sight of navy blue, and Ethan knew it. Too bad that time wasn't now. She shoved her long hair inside as Ethan pounded on the door.

In the hallway, he grabbed her wrist and pulled her behind him as he raced for the stairs, phone to his ear. "Status?" They pushed through the door as he repeated what he was hearing. "Stairway is clear to the lobby and it's wide open after that to the truck. Mitch set up a secondary safe house in town with an army buddy who won't ask questions. It will do until I arrange a more secure place." He looked over his shoulder as they took the stairs at full speed. "Can you handle this?"

Ashley's muscles screamed, but she nodded. What choice did she have? She could curl up on the landing and give her body a break, but it would be temporary until those men caught her and did so much worse.

At the exit to the lobby Ethan stopped and put his phone to his ear. "Mitch. We're at the lobby stairs. Where are you?"

There was a muffled voice from the other end. Ashley barely made out the words as Ethan pulled the phone away from her ear to let her listen. "Emergency lot. Got two guys checking out vehicles. Security says one in the hospital behaving suspiciously. Lobby's clear. Get where I told you to go. I'll meet you there."

Ethan shoved his phone into his coat pocket and peered out the door, surveying the hallway before he eased Ashley through, scanning as he went, one hand at his hip, one grasping her wrist.

Ashley slipped her hand through to clasp his fingers, seeking to cling to rather than be dragged. She'd rather trust anyone other than the man who'd turned her life upside down twice but, right now, Ethan Kincaid was all she had.

There had been many assignments. Many people to protect…including himself. But Ethan's pulse had never pounded the way it was right now. This wasn't just a mission. It was Ashley.

He glanced behind them. No one followed.

God, is this my second chance to make up for what I wrecked the first time?

Did God even operate that way? Doubtful, but Ethan sure wasn't going to allow death near Ashley yet again.

At the lobby entrance, Ethan stopped and scanned the large, open area. A security guard sat at the main desk, but the rest of the room was silent. Too early for visitors. Hopefully, the guard had already been alerted that they'd be passing through. A shout, a radio call, a holdup now could put them in the crosshairs.

He glanced at Ashley and met her eyes for the first time since he'd told her the whole story.

Her gaze didn't waver.

Ethan readied himself to run, struck by the sheer power she must have locked inside if she could hold it together in the face of panic and betrayal and danger this way. She wasn't as weak as she thought.

"Ready?"

Ashley gave one curt nod, much as she had the day they'd split up at the front of that military duplex.

Ethan didn't let the similarity rattle him. He couldn't. With one more sweep of the empty lobby, he hustled her across, careful to keep her at his side, her ball cap low. The cap. She'd likely hit him with it when things slowed down, but he hadn't been able to resist when the helpful nurse pulled her gym bag from her locker, even in light of the long, rocky, uphill road they still had to climb.

The guard looked up, tossed a salute their way and watched them go. Ethan allowed himself a small jolt of relief. Their smallest hurdle was cleared. Now to get to his truck and out of the hospital parking lot. He wouldn't rest easy until they were ten miles from here with no headlights behind them.

The lobby doors swished open, revealing the rapidly increasing light of predawn. Too much light and not nearly enough shadow for them to hide as they crossed the open space.

There was no time to stop now.

Ethan ran for his vehicle and pulled Ashley behind him as fast as her legs would let him. He listened for the sounds of shouts, gunfire—anything that said they'd been spotted.

But there was nothing.

He didn't dare look back to find out why.

He released Ashley when they reached the truck so he could click the lock and she could dive into the passenger seat.

Ashley stayed low as Ethan hit the driver's seat, key in the ignition before he'd even settled in. The engine roared to life as Ethan scanned the parking lot.

Nothing moved. No sound broke the silence. Whoever was looking for them must still be searching.

He was out of the parking lot and on the main road before he dared to look at Ashley.

She clutched the seat so tightly, her knuckles whitened, but at least it seemed her mind had stopped racing. Maybe this time he wouldn't find himself behind another gas station waiting for her panic to pass. There wasn't time to stop. "You okay?"

She nodded tightly. "I have to be."

Ethan said a silent prayer for her, snapped his seat belt into place and then reached for his phone.

His partner answered with a curse. "Bad timing, Kincaid. You'd better be calling to tell me you're clear and on your way to that address."

"Status?"

"Negative."

The word nearly stopped Ethan's heart. Mitch was in trouble. His foot lifted from the accelerator. They had to go back. His eyes found Ashley's. No, he had to get her to safety. He was trapped between competing goals.

"Mitch…"

"Get the girl out of here, Kincaid. We'll link up at the—" There was a shout, the sound of a distant gunshot and the thud of a phone crashing to the ground.

"Mitch!" Ethan shouted the name and Ashley jumped. *Please, God, don't let Mitch be the one down.*

There was a rustle and then breathing on the line.

"Thank You, Lord." He'd said the prayer out loud before he thought it. "What's going on, Mitch?"

"Captain Kincaid. Your partner is—" A close gunshot. Ethan flinched, muscles threatening to explode from his skin. "Sadly, your partner is dead. And when we find you, you will need the God you were praying to."

The line died.

The truck rocked as Ethan slammed on the brakes, opened the window and hurled the phone, putting distance between them and the compromised device. Right there, sitting in the middle of a residential street, he jammed the truck into Park and pounded the steering wheel with his fist. Not. Again.

Not another partner.

Not Mitch.

The world fogged red in anger and pain. He'd go back. He'd find the man on the other end of Mitch's phone. He'd—

"Ethan?" Ashley's voice cleared the fog, drew him to why he was here. He couldn't mourn now. Couldn't let emotion cloud his judgment. He was on his own, the only one who could save Ashley and Sean.

The only one who could bring down the men who'd killed his partners.

He fought to control his breathing. In. Out. Hold. The way he'd learned to steady his hand on the firing range. This was combat. Combat didn't stop for pain.

"Ethan?" This time she laid her hand on his arm.

He forced himself to relax, to pull his arm from her touch, because what he really wanted to do was to reach over and pull her close, to shield her while she comforted him. He wanted to feel her living warmth more than he wanted to survive the next ten minutes. And that would never do.

How did he answer her question? Lie? Again?

She'd know, and she'd never trust him again, especially not after all she'd learned this night.

Ethan rolled up the window and eased his truck into Drive, intent on where to go next. Without Mitch, there was no way to know that his friend's place was secure.

Yes, it was the plan, but the plan had changed. Now his only other choice was a location he hadn't yet secured. He swallowed hard and opted to tell the truth.

"Agent Mitchum is dead."

NINE

Ashley dug her fingernails into the leather seat as the sky streaked brighter, light chasing darkness.

In her life, dark swallowed light faster than she could outrun it.

Dead.

Mitchum had died protecting her.

Ethan's words mingled with a long-remembered scenario that had rocketed her life in a totally unwanted direction. The vision, of Ethan holding her while she stared at her own blood on her hands, grew bolder and bolder.

Cold sweat prickled her hot skin. Nausea rolled over her in waves. She pressed her thumbs into her thighs, trying to find something to hold on to. They couldn't stop for her to panic while they had no idea if they were being followed.

She was trapped.

"Ethan..."

It took a moment before her voice broke. When it did, he was slow to turn his attention from the road. Once he focused, the look of concern humiliated her and called to her all at the same time.

She needed him.

It hit with a rush that outran the panic. When she was clinging to life, she'd reached for him. When she was in the hospital tonight, she'd wanted him. The very idea put the brakes on her fear in a way nothing else ever had.

Ethan reached for her hand and pulled it between them, holding tight. "Focus. And hang on. You're going to be okay."

For the first time she believed him. At his touch, she calmed, as though she'd been looking for that anchor the entire time, not realizing what she was floundering for. He was her safe place. Not her home. Not her job. Not anything but him. And he always had been.

That was the problem.

Ashley pulled away and clasped her hands between her knees, trying to use her own cold fingers to erase the warmth of his touch. Ethan wasn't known for sticking around, was used to bouncing from place to place. And now? With this new job to pull him all around the world? He wouldn't stand still and wait for her, a woman of no use to him, who couldn't give him anything because she was so wrapped up in herself, too scared to live outside her predefined, protected boxes.

And then there was God, who seemed to delight in taking her security.

She pulled her arms tight around her abdomen, her finger brushing the scar on her left side. No. She was better off without him, even though she wanted him more than she wanted to live to see the rest of this day.

"Talk to me." Ethan's voice drifted low, as if he recognized he faced a volatile creature in the seat beside him. "You going to make it?"

He didn't say they couldn't pull over right now, and she was grateful. If he had, the panic would have resurged, had her trapped until she was a wild thing trying to leap from the moving vehicle.

"I'm fine." Focus on Ethan. Not on herself. "How are

you? Mitchum. Your…partner." His new partner. Her heart ached for him. Ethan's life was as out of control as hers was, no matter how much he pretended he had the situation covered. His trusted, longtime partner Jacob had been murdered. His new partner was dead. Sean was missing.

He was the last man standing.

"I don't have time to think about it now. If I do, I'll turn this truck around, and he'd never forgive me for taking you back into the hands of those men and making his death be in vain." Ethan didn't look at her. He just kept driving, putting miles between them and the hospital. Between them and his partner. "We've got another problem."

Not more problems. Why couldn't they just go get the drives, determine the cipher key, pass the intel on to the people searching for Sean and get this over with?

"I don't have anywhere to take you."

The tension in her face melted with the shock of the statement. "What?" Her jaw worked back and forth, as though it needed to build the strength to ask the next question, as though it was afraid the answer wouldn't be the one she wanted. "I thought… The safe house?"

"It's been compromised." He ran his tongue over his teeth. "One of the last things Mitchum said to me was someone had ransacked it. Whether it was the guys after you or a poorly timed coincidence, I can't take the risk of having you near that place."

Ashley moved to speak, but Ethan held up a hand. "I have another idea, but I have to make some phone calls and, well…" His smile was rueful. "That's going to be hard until I can pick up another phone. I can't take you there until I know it's safe."

"Where?" She needed to know, to readjust her thinking so she could prepare herself. The unexpected was her worst nightmare, and one she'd been living with for the past eight hours in a way she'd never imagined.

"Can't tell you yet. For now, we need to get as far from here and as close to Black River as we can. And I need somewhere to pay cash for a phone."

Ashley's mind raced. Safety. They needed a place to lie low. "What kind of place?"

"Somewhere out of the way, where not too many people will spot you."

For the first time in what felt like her entire life, a grin tilted the corners of Ashley's lips. "I think I know the place." Familiar, comfortable… A place where she could find some peace.

Ethan studied her as though he was gauging her sincerity and could trust her judgment. His jaw relaxed. "Tell me where to go."

Few things in the world were more nerve-racking than driving up cold to a place on which he possessed no intel, but Ethan had no choice. He needed sleep and some time to regroup, and so did Ashley. As the sun moved higher in the sky, fatigue deepened the lines on her face. Twice, her head nodded, but she caught herself before sleep claimed her, her vigilance rivaling his own.

Small twigs popped under the tires as they wound up the wooded drive leading to Ashley's grandparents' vacation cabin. Through the bare branches, sunlight sparkled off of the St. Lawrence River, tingeing the trees in a glow. Even with the windows up, the earthy scent of spring filtered into the truck.

Beside him, Ashley stirred in her seat, her face softening as they drove deeper into the woods. "We used to come spend our summers here as kids." She pointed high up to the right where a platform clung precariously to a tree. "Sean and his dad used to go hunting with my dad. That's one of the tree stands they used to sit in to watch for deer. Those trips could keep us fed most of the winter."

Her voice cracked and Ethan slowed the vehicle, reaching for her hand. He stopped short at one more reminder of what she shared with Sean. It was a past he couldn't touch. This couldn't be easy for her. The memories of her parents and Sean's, who'd died together in a car accident shortly after she'd joined the army...of Sean himself, whose life could already be over.

Ethan grabbed the cell phone that lay on the seat between them. They'd stopped at a twenty-four-hour superstore and picked up a prepaid burner phone and a laptop for Ashley. She'd spent half of the ride north disabling the wireless capabilities. It had given her something to focus on, probably kept her from having another attack on the drive. How many could one person endure in one night?

His fingers ached to dial the phone to his superiors, but he was hesitant. The compromised safe house, Mitch's warning and Sean's disappearance... With every step, it was clear that someone was working on the inside, listening in on their most secure lines. It was too risky. If he could just link up with his buddy Tate Walker, make sure Tate's house was free, he'd have access. But Tate wasn't answering, which bothered him as much as anything else.

No, Ethan wasn't ready for someone to track them yet. He needed rest first. "You're sure there's no way to trace this place to you?"

"Am I sure of anything?" Ashley smoothed her hands across the dash of the truck, launching fine dust particles into the light. "It's been in my family since before the Civil War. Everything is in the name of my extended family on my mother's side. If anyone's looking for us, they're going to have to do some digging and it will take time."

Ethan suppressed a groan. Yeah, it would take time, but it seemed these guys' connections ran deeper at every turn. How long would it take them to trace Ashley's family tree, if they hadn't already?

The cabin came into view. The sprawling log structure looked like everything he'd envisioned a cabin in the North Country to be, but larger. The original structure was obvious, the logs rougher than some of the additions, the newer green tin roof glowing in the mottled sunlight.

Set back from the road, buried in trees… If Ethan had ordered a safe house, this would be as close to perfect as it would come.

Ashley exhaled, the tension almost visibly pouring from her body. "I need to sleep. For a very long time." She angled her neck to one side, then the other, wincing.

"How are you feeling?" She hadn't complained once since they'd left the hospital, but fatigue and on-setting pain were probably tugging hard.

"Sore. Nothing some rest won't improve, although I probably won't be saying that when I wake up."

Ethan started to smile but a flash of metal around the corner of the cabin caught his attention. His short-lived peace fled. "Somebody's here."

Instantly, Ashley leaned forward, her hands splayed against the dash.

Panic thrived on exhaustion and he was certain Ashley was at the very edge of her reserves.

Please, Lord, don't let peace be dangled in front of her and jerked away before she can rest.

The back end of a car came into view and Ethan jammed on the brakes, preparing to hit Reverse and floor it until they were on the road going…where?

Ashley's warm hand on his arm stopped him. "I know that car."

"You're sure?"

"It's my cousin Katrina. She's an accountant, helps me with the books sometimes, though I'm not sure why she's here. It's the height of tax season for her. Last time we talked, she was bunking with her parents because a pipe burst in her apartment and flooded her out."

Ethan tried to hit Snooze on the alarm ringing in his head. Fatigue and being found too many times had charged his wariness up to eleven. "We need to leave." Whether Katrina was trustworthy or not, he couldn't risk getting one more person involved in a situation so volatile that bodies were falling on every side.

"No, we don't."

Ethan shook his head but Ashley ignored him. "Katrina's my cousin. I've known her my whole life. She's no threat."

"It's not her I'm worried about. It's what happens if someone finds us and shows up here." Then he'd have two people whose lives depended on him.

Ashley rolled her eyes. "What other choice do we have? Both of us are going to drop dead from exhaustion if we don't do something."

Ethan ground his teeth together. He pulled in behind the small sedan and shifted his truck into Park, hand shaking with fatigue. He was at his limit, no good to anybody if he didn't get some rest soon.

Ashley was right. What choice did they have?

Rolling onto her side, Ashley buried her face in the depths of her pillow, trying to shake off the dream that wakefulness had pulled her from. She squeezed her eyes tight, willing away the image of Ethan and Sean unmoving, bleeding into the grass as she tried to save them, her own blood staining the ground.

She rolled over onto her back. Sunlight poured in through the square-paned windows, fairy dust dancing in the beams. For one second it was easy to believe she was a small child again, waking from the nap she'd always hated while her grandmother baked cookies in the kitchen.

Until she stretched her arms over her head. Every part of her body ached, even her little toe. She lay there, staring at the wood planks of the ceiling, taking inventory. Yep. Every muscle hurt.

But she still felt better than before she'd lain down. She'd thank God for the sleep, if He was still listening to her.

She'd prayed every night for her parents to be safe; prayed as she'd rounded the corner of the military duplex that they'd all come out okay; prayed for her future in the military. He'd flat-out ignored her every time. With Sean missing and terrorists on her trail, it was obvious God had fed her to the lions.

"You feeling any better?" The low female voice jerked Ashley to sitting, screaming pain straight into her fingertips. She winced as she found her cousin peeking in the doorway.

Katrina frowned and acted as though she might duck right back out of the room again. "Sorry. I heard you moving around and wanted to see if you needed anything. You've been out for a while."

"I'm fine. I doubt my body will feel the same for a very long time after last night, though."

Blond hair fell forward as Katrina tipped her head, looking for all the world like the puppy Ashley had once adopted.

It was Ashley's turn to frown. Katrina knew nothing

other than Ashley and Ethan needed a place to crash. Now Ashley had tipped her cousin off that there was more to the story. A story she had no idea how much of which she could tell.

The less, the better.

Katrina motioned with her hand toward the foot of the bed and Ashley nodded her assent, tugging at her sweat-shirt and pulling the comforter taut beneath her. She'd collapsed on the bed without even bothering to unmake it and slept for…how long? A shower and the change of clothes she'd picked up on their dash through the super-store last night would be bliss.

Picking up the baseball cap Ashley had tossed onto the floor, Katrina ran a thumb along the bill and lifted an eyebrow. "Yankees? You're a die-hard member of the Red Sox Nation despite our best efforts to bring you around to the home team."

"I'm a rebel. What can I say?" Ashley reached for the cap and tapped the white logo. "Ethan thought it was funny, I guess."

Sinking onto the edge of the bed, Katrina leveled a motherly gaze on Ashley. Three years older than Ashley, Katrina had never missed a chance to hold her "matu-rity" over her cousin. "So…" She tugged a wrinkle out of the comforter by Ashley's foot. "Tell me about you and Ethan."

Not the question Ashley had expected…and definitely not one she was prepared to answer.

She shrugged, shoulders and neck protesting. "There's no 'me and Ethan.' He's an old friend of mine and Sean's." It was the truth, but not all of it. Her respect for Ethan notched up a bit. This was how he must have felt hav-ing to parcel out information throughout the night. It wasn't easy.

"Sean. I don't think I've seen him since you two broke off your engagement. You guys were always together when we were growing up. Used to make me jealous."

"I'm sorry." It was true. Whenever Sean's family had joined them on vacation, Ashley and he had gravitated toward one another, the outdoor enthusiasts in the group, while Katrina had stayed inside and kept her fingernails clean. "It wasn't on purpose."

Katrina waved a perfectly manicured hand. "Fine by me. I got all of Grandma's attention." She winked. "Blew my mind when you two broke it off. Everybody assumed you'd get married, have a million children and walk right into being grown-ups just like you were as kids."

"Never would have worked. We knew each other too well. We were brought up too much like brother and sister to see each other as anything else." The affection between them was a lasting bond, but it lacked the passion that led to the kind of love needed for a marriage. Kissing Sean had never felt right, so they almost never did. Ethan, on the other hand... Just the thought of kissing him curled her toes.

"Too bad. He's a great guy. Used to treat you the way I'm still looking for someone to treat me."

"Never said we didn't love each other, just that it was the wrong kind of love to hold a marriage together."

"He still single?" Katrina's eyebrows waggled.

It would have been funny under other circumstances. "He's deployed." *Leave it at that.* "What time is it anyway?"

"About two in the afternoon. You've been out for a few hours, and Ethan is still asleep in the other room. What dragged you guys up here?"

Katrina hadn't asked many questions when they'd staggered into the house. She'd just said she'd sought solitude at the cabin. Fortunately for them, she'd been grocery shopping and, after bacon and eggs, Ashley had fallen on top of the quilt, still in her clothes, in the room she'd always thought of as her own.

At the memory of breakfast Ashley's stomach rumbled and Katrina's smile widened. "I'll feed you if you tell me the truth. I put venison in the slow cooker. Grandpa left some in the freezer."

Ashley settled against the pillows, lace tickling her neck, and let her mouth water. Venison. When was the last time she'd had the staple from her childhood? "With gravy? And rice?" It did her mind good to talk about something other than thumb drives and cyber terrorists, but she wasn't sure how long Katrina would be put off.

"No rice. But salt potatoes."

Salt potatoes. The upstate delicacy of potatoes soaked in brine, boiled and tossed in butter was one Ashley hadn't eaten in years. If Katrina kept listing her favorite comfort foods and asking questions, Ashley would sell Ethan and the whole operation out before dinner.

Katrina tipped her head to the side. "Wait… Ethan. I know that name."

Ashley tried to keep her face from betraying any emotion. Maybe Katrina's memory was bad. She was the oldest, after all.

Her cousin snapped her fingers. No such luck. "I thought he looked familiar. He was at the hospital the day you were…" Katrina waved off the thought and picked at a knot in the floral quilt. "You know, that day… I really thought you were gone. And there was that guy. Ethan… Kincaid, right?" She didn't wait for Ashley to answer. "Ethan Kincaid. Standing there fresh out of the ambulance, covered in…" She looked up at Ashley with a sad smile. "He was more shaken up than I've ever seen any man. At the time, I thought maybe he was..."

She sniffed and brushed away the rest of the words like a fly. "And now here you two show up out of nowhere, both looking like you haven't slept in weeks and you moving like an eighty-year-old. There's some explaining to do here, dear cousin."

No, there wasn't. Ashley schooled her face into impassivity, but what she really wanted was to grab her cousin by the collar and drag out the rest of the sentence she hadn't finished. She thought Ethan was what? It had never occurred to Ashley to ask him how he'd felt with her bleeding out in his arms. She'd never known he rode to the hospital with her, just assumed he'd followed in one of their squad cars. The knowledge cast a new light on that day, one she wanted to ask about, but one she knew better than to touch. There needed to be a distance between them if she wanted to avoid getting her heart broken again when he left for parts unknown.

Katrina was oblivious to Ashley's thoughts. "How did you wind up with him?"

Ashley licked dry lips and fought to keep her eyes on her cousin. If she looked away, it would be a tell that she wasn't putting forth the whole truth. "He needed my help analyzing some files and we needed a place to work that was neutral ground." At least she hadn't lied.

"And you're walking like an old woman because...?"

"Hit-and-run. Someone totaled my car with me in it, but I'm fine. Nothing a few days' rest won't cure." If she was lucky enough to get a few days of rest. As soon as Ethan lined up another safe house, they'd be out of this cabin, the one sense of home she had left.

"Hit-and-run? When?" Katrina pulled Ashley's hand toward her. "How many lives do you have?"

Ashley pulled her fingers from her cousin's and tried to smile at what Katrina thought was a joke. The truth was, no matter how large the number was to start, it was likely dwindling fast.

TEN

Ethan sat straight up on the bed and reached for his gun on the nightstand by instinct, fighting to remember where he was. It took a few moments before he comprehended the heavy log walls around him and the brightly colored quilt beneath him. The warm scent of heavily spiced meat drifted into the room.

Ashley's grandparents' cabin.

Ashley.

He searched for the clock—3:11? In the afternoon? How had he fallen asleep? He was supposed to be vigilant, taking an hour-long power nap not a daylong break from the action. If anything had happened to her...

Forcing himself to calm down, he sat back on the bed. Silence reigned in the room and the air hung coolly around him, streaked by late-day sun. From the other side of the closed door, soft voices drifted, a quiet chuckle mingled with a slight giggle. The girls sounded fine, and the downtime would help Ashley, hopefully give her the strength she needed to keep moving until this thing was over.

In the solitude of the small guest room, Ethan rested his head against the headboard and stared at the tongue-and-groove ceiling, forcing himself to trust in the God he couldn't see on the other side, the God who'd gotten him through Ashley's near-death experience and through countless other situations he didn't care to recall. Cut off from his superiors with his partner dead, the helplessness was almost overwhelming, driving him into the arms of the only One he could depend on.

He forced his eyes to stay open so his mind wouldn't paint a picture of what had happened on the other side of that phone. Mitchum was a pain in the neck sometimes, but he was one of the best agents Ethan had ever worked with. The grief slammed him right in the chest. If only he could go to Ashley and hold her until he forgot the hurt.

Lord, you've got to watch out for Ashley. God alone could do that, and it would do well for Ethan never to forget it. *I need her.*

There was the plea he hadn't wanted to leak out. The words that shattered the lies he'd been telling himself. He'd never stopped loving Ashley Colson. He'd run from her, knowing five years ago he could never give her what she needed, had in fact taken what she wanted. He'd gone to the ends of the earth, sunk himself into missions, given everything he possessed to his job and yet…it wasn't enough. Last night, looking her square in the eye in the back of Mitch's truck after rescuing her, he'd known it, even if he'd been denying it ever since.

Ethan let a groan escape. None of it mattered. He could feel about her any way he wanted, but he couldn't act. Ashley was vulnerable, in a place where she needed stability, someone who could pull her close and understand her without words. She needed someone like Sean, who shared her pain and her triumphs. The last thing she needed was a man driven by his conscience to fight the enemies of his country.

She needed Ethan to shutter his heart so he could protect her without his emotions clouding his instincts.

As much as he felt for Ashley, she was better off without him. He'd keep doing what he'd been doing, moving from place to place, seeking out the bad guys. This time could be no different from any other. He needed to remember that or he'd lose focus, and lost focus would get Ashley and him both killed.

Thinking about it any more would keep him from finishing the job. He needed a shower and clean clothes and then they needed to make the short drive to the post office as soon as darkness settled. At this time of year, that was only a couple of hours away.

Ethan was towel drying his hair and rejoicing in the feel of clean clothes as only a man who had been in combat could when the shrill ring of a cell phone silenced the voices in the next room. He balled the towel up and tossed it on the bed. Surely, Ashley wouldn't...

But it wasn't her voice that called a hello. Katrina's vaguely familiar lilt filtered through the door, punctuated by her footfalls as she walked toward what must be her bedroom. "Hello, Sam. I'm missing a few of the documents I need to complete your company's taxes. No, you didn't interrupt anything other than a catch-up session with my cousin." He heard her muffled voice as a door closed and stillness reigned again.

Ethan exhaled relief. He didn't know Katrina well and didn't relish having to explain details to her that might run contrary to what Ashley had already told her.

Besides, seeing her brought memories. It was only when he was nearly asleep earlier that her face had gelled in his mind, creased with fear and streaked with tears in the waiting room after Ashley's shooting. He dragged a finger along the scar next to his eye, the one inflicted when he'd tackled the shooter and been rewarded with a fist to the face. It was probably a good thing the man had landed that blow, because had Ethan gained the upper hand in his blind rage, he might have killed him.

The blow left the scar he saw every day, a reminder of his loss. But Ethan's charge had slowed the guy down enough for backup to catch him hiding in a garage two streets over.

Ethan pulled the door open gently and was greeted with the sight of Ashley in profile, feet curled under her on the dark leather love seat, steaming mug cradled between her hands as she stared out the floor-to-ceiling windows that faced the river.

Those would never work if this was a real safe house.

But that thought evaporated at the sight of her, semi-relaxed for the first time in this whole ordeal. He could get used to this, walking into a room and catching her unaware, a look of contentment on her face. The crackle of the wood in the fireplace and the warmth of bright, hooked rugs nearly undid his tongue, made him want to confess that this was what he wanted every day for the rest of his life.

The change in his breathing must have been audible because she looked up and smiled. "Sleep well?"

She never should have asked him something so normal. It drove the desire for more moments when this could be their every morning. "Too well. You?" It was lame, stupid, and it had better not sound as choked to her ears as it did to his. This was ridiculous. He was a soldier, assigned to take down terrorists, to find Sean and to rescue her.

Sitting beside her would make it worse, especially on the two-person love seat, but he couldn't stop himself. He needed to feel alive, to be close to her more than he needed to eat or sleep. He needed a few moments of peace in a world where people were missing and dying, dependent on him to keep them safe, and he was failing them.

"Ethan?" Ashley settled her mug on the heavy wooden coffee table, the earthy scent of black coffee trailing in its wake and curdling Ethan's stomach. "What's wrong?" She scanned the broad windows over her shoulder, fear edging into her expression. "Did you see something?"

He swallowed hard, anger bubbling in his gut. He'd wrecked the moment. "Nothing. Just..." He couldn't lie to her. "Thinking too hard."

"Something I'm trying to avoid." She studied him for another moment then picked up her mug and cradled it again, leaning against the seat cushions, leaving Ethan free to study her profile. "I'm pretending I'm an ostrich. For a little bit, I'm sticking my head in the sand." She took a sip of coffee. "Guess that's one of the benefits of the past five years. I've learned to fool myself into thinking everything's okay even when it's not."

"As long as you don't crawl into your head and live there forever."

"It's tempting." She angled her body toward him, leaning her shoulder against the back of the love seat. Her knee brushed his thigh, shooting a whole different kind of twist into his stomach. She was close enough to touch and still a million miles away. "No matter how hard I try, though, I can't stop thinking about Mitchum. He..." Tears welled in those translucent green eyes. "He suffered what I did, but his didn't end as well. He didn't have..." Her mouth snapped shut, eyes widening as they glistened with unshed tears.

You. The unspoken word pounded against Ethan's skull. *He didn't have you.*

They'd followed protocol last night, done what they were supposed to do to protect their charge. Guilt washed through Ethan's stomach and blended with grief in a cocktail he wished he'd never had to drink. There was nothing he could have done to save Mitch. Had he had Mitch's back, they'd both be dead and Ashley would be in the hands of those men, her fate and Sean's sealed.

When he looked up, Ashley was staring at him, searching every inch of his face. She lowered her mug to the couch and held it tight. "I never knew you rode in the ambulance with me the first time." Her voice was low and soft, full of something he didn't need to hear.

Yet he couldn't stop listening. "I couldn't let you go alone. I couldn't let you..." *Die alone.* "I needed to be there and to know you were going to be okay." Without thinking, he reached forward, fingertips brushing her cheek, to slip a stray lock of hair behind her ear. It was still damp from her shower, smelling like apples and something he couldn't identify but that he'd always attached to her.

When her lips parted, he knew he was going to kiss her. Even though the rational part of him screamed that this was the worst thing he could do. Once he did, there was no going back, no way he'd ever untangle himself from the emotions he'd fallen into since the first day he'd laid eyes on her in formation at Fort Drum. Posture perfect, hair tucked under her patrol cap, Ashley had always had a focused determination that drew him. She ran through his veins in a way he couldn't defy.

And if her eyes could be trusted, the same thing was happening to her.

He let his hand drift into the soft hair along the back of her neck and waited for her to give him permission.

She leaned closer, eyes drifting shut, warm breath brushing his cheek, inviting him to close that last breath between them.

The bedroom door clicked open and Katrina's voice drifted out. "That was easier than I thought."

Ethan dropped his hand and retreated, fingers cold from the contrast of touching her.

Ashley stared at him, as shell-shocked as any soldier he'd ever seen, fingers limp around the coffee mug she still held in her lap.

Ethan pushed up from the love seat, feeling the tear as he looked down at her, the regret in her expression probably the mirror image of his own, only his was tinged with guilt. "That can't happen, Ash."

He left her, mentally kicking himself all the way to the kitchen. God had stopped him from making what would have been the biggest mistake of his life, the same mistake that had nearly killed her the last time.

Ashley watched Ethan walk into the kitchen, where he kept his back to her as he poured a glass of orange juice then stepped through the doors to the porch. He stared at the St. Lawrence River winding behind the house before pulling his newest phone out of his pocket.

He never looked back.

What couldn't happen? He couldn't be with a woman as weak as her? The fire in her veins blew from desire to anger. That was just like him. To make her need him and then walk away, leaving her to deal with the aftermath. To turn away when she needed him to be her rock.

Ashley stood and took two steps toward the door, ready to demand answers.

Except it wasn't true. Ignoring Katrina's presence, Ashley sank to the love seat. She pulled her grandmother's crocheted afghan from behind her, curling up inside it as though it could replace the warmth Ethan had taken with him. Ethan hadn't left her. He'd been beside her all the way to the hospital, had revealed something in that waiting room that even Katrina had been able to read.

Ashley watched him over her shoulder, his back a wall between them. More than anything, she wanted to go to him, to find out what had driven him to her side that day and what drove him away from her now, but she couldn't. There was only so much rejection a girl could handle in the space of five minutes.

The cushions sank as Katrina dropped into the spot Ethan had vacated. When Ashley turned, Katrina was watching him. "He's gorgeous, you know."

Oh, yeah, Ashley knew. With that sandy-blond hair that curled at the ends, those brown eyes that looked right through her and those shoulders under that green sweater. Yeah, he was beyond easy to look at. But that gorgeousness was clearly wrapped around a man she could never have. "If you're into silent and distant."

Katrina chuckled and reached for her coffee mug, grimacing as she took a sip of what was likely cold brew. "Look, my questions were out of line earlier. You've been friends so long, you two are probably more like brother and sister, like you and Sean, huh?"

Was she fishing to see if Ethan was available? Surely not. Katrina wasn't the type to chase a guy. Men flocked to her classic beauty, but her standards were high. Still, she'd hinted at loneliness, so it wasn't out of the realm of possibility.

"He's unavailable." Ashley bit off the words. Let Katrina take whatever meaning she wanted.

Katrina arched a knowing eyebrow. "Maybe I was wrong?"

"About what?"

She shrugged and started to say something else.

Ashley cut her off. Nothing Katrina said would make

one bit of difference in her emotions or Ethan's. "What was your phone call about?" It was nosy, but it would change the subject.

"Oh." Katrina toed the phone she'd settled on the coffee table and edged it as far from her as she could stretch. "Client claimed he'd sent me his statements for his overseas accounts when I knew he hadn't. Five minutes of tinkering with his email and he found the information in an unsent email. It happens pretty regularly, and investment companies seem to be the worst. Sometimes I think they understand numbers but not much else."

"I know. Been there before, but usually when it comes time for me to get paid."

The door slipped open but Ashley refused to look over her shoulder. The air almost crackled, as though even oxygen was aware there was something different about Ethan Kincaid.

Katrina looked up. "I was telling Ash here that I threw some venison in the slow cooker while you two were sleeping. You should have seen her eyes light up."

"Sounds good." Ethan cleared his throat. "But we won't be here for dinner. Sorry."

Ashley whipped around so fast her neck protested and coffee sloshed on her wrist. "What?" Her mind revved to cue her body into flight. They were safe here. No one knew where they were; they were safe in a home base; she was comfortable in familiar surroundings. Now he wanted to drag her into the unknown again? "Where are we going?"

Ethan fired a warning glance toward Katrina, who was sputtering a protest about how they'd just gotten there. "We have some mail to pick up." He leveled a *you-should-know-this* gaze on Ashley.

Mail to pick up. In the shock about Mitchum, Ashley

had nearly forgotten the thumb drives. Sean was never far from her mind, but the fact there was a job to do had melted away with a solid nap and a warm cup of coffee.

Ashley stood, the afghan she'd pulled over her legs dropping in a puddle to the floor. "When?"

"We're pulling out as soon as it gets dark." He looked away from her to Katrina. "Thanks for having us." Without another word, he disappeared into his room and shut the door.

Katrina whistled low. "Wow. He's intense, isn't he?"

Ashley shook her head, staring at the closed door, its solid *thunk* a reminder there would always be something between them.

ELEVEN

Ethan willed his foot to stay level on the gas pedal as the Black River Post Office came into view. Slowing would call unwanted attention. They had ten minutes until the lobby closed, so time for surveillance ticked short.

He'd finally reached Tate Walker. His place was empty and waiting for them to arrive, and Ethan was anxious to get there, the one place he should be able to send a secure message to higher-up.

He scanned the parking lot of the small Dollar General next to the post office, where three vehicles were parked. All appeared to be empty and none gave him a twinge of familiarity. No cars sat in the post-office parking lot, though Ethan didn't like the stand of trees running along the right side and behind the building. At least the square brick building offered few places to hide and the columns at the front were too small to shield a man.

The open layout was small comfort. He eyed the trees as they passed, looking for anything out of place, though the lack of streetlights in the early evening made movement hard to discern. They'd have to risk it. He glanced in the rearview mirror to make sure no one was behind them and scanned the drivers pumping gas at a nearby gas station.

None even looked up as he passed.

Ethan drove farther up the road and turned around at a small trailer park where shadows moved in the breeze. It was now or never. If they waited another day, someone else might get there first…if they hadn't already.

Ashley sat straight in the seat beside him, watching everything except him. She'd been distant ever since their brief encounter earlier and her silence sliced at his soul. She was probably angry he'd betrayed both her and Sean with that near kiss. Still, whether it was what he wanted or not, their relationship was best this way.

"Doing okay?" He'd seen the way she held the post-box key in her hand, so tight it was bound to be biting into her flesh.

"As okay as I'm going to be. I'll feel better once we're at your safe house and I can make sure Sean really did leave us a cipher to unlock his files." She was doing that thing he couldn't understand, staying level in the face of danger, almost as though she couldn't dare to acknowledge one iota of emotion or the panic would consume her. That took more strength than she'd ever realize.

Being in the truck on the move made even his trained mind feel exposed and vulnerable. He couldn't begin to imagine how it twisted emotions already prone to fear. "Here's what we'll do." There was no good way to pull this off, but he'd thought through every scenario. If he'd have been comfortable doing it, he'd have left her at the cabin, where she'd be relatively safe, but having her out of his sight for nearly an hour and a half while he made the run to Black River and back made him uneasy. "You duck below the level of the windows and lock the door behind me. I'll go—"

"You will do no such thing. I'm not staying out here exposed while you go in there by yourself."

"Ashley, I have no idea who's in that building. For all I know, they've beat us here and are waiting for you to show up with the key."

"Or they beat us here and are hiding in those woods to drag me out of the truck when your back is turned." She aimed a finger at him. "I know you've gone a whole lot farther in your training than I did, but there are things I remember. Either we both go or neither of us goes."

He'd let her override his plans at the airport and that certainly hadn't ended well. History repeating itself left a metallic taste in his mouth. "Ashley…"

"I'm safer with you than without you."

The words slammed into his chest. After all that had happened, she believed that? Her trust sealed the deal. "Okay, but you do everything I say without question. Understood?"

"Yes."

Ethan's muscles coiled as the truck eased to a stop in the space closest to the entrance. "I don't like how I can't see into those woods. Crawl over and get out on my side."

Nothing but leaves moved in the small bit of dim light he could see in the trees. He glanced at the Dollar General parking lot. A tall man dressed in full garb against the chill that lingered into early spring exited and headed at a rapid pace toward his white sedan. Multiple bags hunched the man's shoulders.

Ethan watched him get in his car and start it before sending a curt nod to Ashley, who waited for his order to move. "Let's go."

He kept his hand at his weapon as she scooted across the front seat and jumped out, her eyes on the front door of the building. This time he didn't touch her, just gestured for her to stay close as they entered through the glass doors.

Ethan paused to listen and heard nothing but their own movements echoing on the tiled floor. Keeping an eye on his truck to ensure no one slipped into it, he stepped backward into the room while Ashley remained behind him. "Where's the box?" He kept his voice low as Ashley gave him the number. It took a moment of searching that stretched into eternity before she found the box midway down around the corner of the lobby.

Ashley inserted the key in the lock and pulled a stack of mail from the slot.

Ethan silently urged her to hurry, keeping his eyes on the truck as she flipped through the mail. Nothing moved in the parking lot.

It hadn't occurred to him the package might be too large to fit in the box, and they may have to get it from the clerk. Without proper ID, a risky face-to-face meeting might—

"Got it." He heard Ashley's muffled voice around the flat, padded envelope she held between her teeth. She shoved the rest of the mail into the slot and slammed the door, slipping the envelope into her inside jacket pocket. "Let's get out of here."

"You're leaving the rest of the mail?"

"If they figure out which post office he's sent them to, let them think we never got here."

Smart girl. Her training had stuck. For the first time Ethan grasped the regret she must swallow every day. She'd have been perfect for missions such as this, her intelligence and computer savvy making her a team leader in no time.

There she went, stealing his focus again. Shaking it off, he nodded toward the door, footfalls echoing. "Let's get out of here. I'll tell you where we're going on the way."

She gave a curt nod and slipped in to his left and a half step behind.

At the exit Ethan scanned the parking lot. Seeing no motion, he pushed through the door and headed for the truck. A few more seconds and—

Thwack. A dull thud and the brick on the column by his head exploded. The retort of a pistol cracked off of the trees.

Ashley gulped a scream, ducking behind him, her body trembling against his back.

Ethan shoved her low behind the mailbox near the front door, pulled his weapon from its holster and crouched behind her, shielding her as best he could. "You okay? Were you hit?"

Ashley curled forward, her face buried in her knees. She didn't respond.

Ethan scanned for wounds and saw none.

Shots fired. This had to be torture for Ashley.

But he couldn't stop to comfort her, as much as he wanted to pull her into his arms and tell her it would all be okay. That was a promise he couldn't make.

Do your job, Kincaid. Glancing up at the damaged brick above him, Ethan traced the bullet trajectory with his eyes. The shot had come from his right. The store next door.

He hazarded a peek between the mailbox and the brick column. The same white sedan sat in its place, engine running, rear window cracked open in defiance of the spring chill.

Silence held court, heavy in the wake of the gun's retort. The guy had fired once. Likely, their pursuer knew he could keep them pinned down as long as he wanted with one shot and minimal attention would be drawn to him. Human nature tended to ignore out-of-place sounds if heard only once, to write them off as something natural. Or, in this neck of the woods, as someone firing off target practice in their backyard.

One of two things was about to happen. If they tried to make an escape, their assailant would open up a barrage of gunfire and run after he'd hit them. Or he'd keep them hunkered down until his buddies arrived to overwhelm them with superior numbers.

Okay. Options.

Ethan could return fire and keep the man occupied to give Ashley the cover she needed to get into the truck. He could shoot out a tire to keep the man from following, but too much gunfire would make Ethan look like the aggressor and there'd be a BOLO issued for his truck before they could get half a mile up the road.

Ethan surveyed the area. They needed an escape route. They could duck into the building, but there was no other easily accessible way out and the postmaster inside would be in danger. If they made it to the truck, he'd likely have two flat tires and a hole in his head before he could put the vehicle in gear and get out of the parking lot. Even if he did make it out of the parking lot, they'd have a tail he couldn't shake.

He gauged the distance between them and the next brick pillar and then peered around the corner. There might be one way out, but it would take everything Ashley had to follow him. And the way she was heaving for air, he wasn't sure the fear would let her.

Ashley pulled herself tighter into a ball, pressing her cheek hard into her knee. There'd be a bruise there tomorrow if she wasn't careful.

Well, if she lived to see tomorrow.

The heat of fear traveled through every pore of her

body. Muscles already aching from last night's attack threatened to seize her into paralysis. Nausea nearly overwhelmed her. *Be where you are right now. Right now. Focus on right now.*

Right now, someone was shooting at her. Right now, her worst nightmare played out in front of her. She could die or, worse, wind up in the hospital, watching the weak structure of her life crumble in more broken dreams. She pulled deeper into herself, body tense as she remembered hot lead entering her body and tearing her insides apart. Her side ached with memory, the sweat on her hands entirely too much like blood.

She squeezed her eyes tighter, but all she could see was blood on her hands, on her uniform, on Ethan's jacket.

She needed to run, needed to get out of here, to get to safety. Anything to get that gun aimed somewhere else.

She clenched her fingers in tight fists as tears leaked down her cheeks. This was bigger than her. She couldn't quit. If she did they'd kill Sean and Ethan and, later, her. Even if they didn't, she'd have to live with the knowledge she'd allowed terrorists to get away with their revenue stream intact, and every day of her life she'd have to watch the news and wonder if her cowardice had funded attacks that cost countless lives.

Ethan leaned forward, his breath close to her right ear. "I have a plan."

Ashley swallowed hard and tried to nod, but she was paralyzed. Why hadn't the gunman fired again? Was he edging closer?

"Stay with me, Colson. We can get out of this. Do you trust me?" The words were so low they were more a feeling than a vocalization, spoken as his head was next to hers in a way that gave him a clear view of the shooter.

Did she trust him? Earlier, she had. He'd failed her

before, but then, as tonight, he'd been right by her side in spite of the danger. And he'd stayed close, saved her life, not left her until he'd known she was safe.

Ashley forced herself to nod. Did she trust him?

With her life.

Ethan seemed to sag against her, his weight heavier for an instant before he pulled slightly away. "Okay. Here's what we do." His left hand snaked around her, finger aimed toward his pickup. "If you stay low, you can get around to the other side of the truck without being seen. If we're quick, we can get across the parking lot and into the woods before he realizes we've moved. The biggest thing you have to worry about is whether or not he can see our feet move, but I doubt it from his angle. The way he's positioned, he can't see us unless we're in the open, and he can't get a clear shot unless he gets out of the car and takes aim, risking multiple witnesses to identify him."

"You really can see him?" Somehow, knowing Ethan had eyes on the shooter gave her the small edge of control she needed. Moving forward would give her more, even if she had to overcome a mile-high wall of fear to get her cramped legs moving in the direction of safety.

"He's in the parking lot next door in a white four-door. Backseat, cracked-open rear window."

Ashley peered in the narrow space and found the vehicle, then glanced in the direction of the woods. Ethan was right. At this angle, they might be able to make it to cover before he realized it.

"We've got to go now, though." Ethan's voice pulled her out of her analysis. "I imagine he's got more hands on the way."

There was only one thing that could scare her more than one gun. Multiple guns. Ashley looked over her shoulder at Ethan, his face close to hers. "Okay."

He didn't break off his surveillance of their assailant. "You can do this, Ash. I believe in you." He flicked a quick, hurried glance at her. "Go and get low where the tire of the truck blocks you from view. I'll cover you." He reached down, squeezed her hand and let go quickly.

Ashley shut her eyes tight and opened them again, focus trained on a small rock behind the truck tire. *Just get to that rock.* All she needed to do was to get to that rock.

Lord, keep us safe. She leaped into motion, eyes on the small, gray rock representing momentary safety.

Her back was pressed against the tire before she realized she'd been tensed the entire time, waiting for a bullet to rip through muscle and tissue. There was nothing but silence and the sounds of distant voices as people left the store next door.

Ethan skidded in beside her, keeping his right hand hidden from her view, likely because he held a weapon he knew she couldn't see. The thought weakened her joints, but she crouched, stared at the tree line and picked out a wide tree that would cover her if the gunman caught sight of them. She didn't dare think of what would happen if he did. They couldn't hide in the narrow strip of trees forever.

· Ethan's chest rose and fell as he studied the trees. "Okay. I can't see him and I can't risk peeking to see if he noticed we moved, but I haven't heard a car door."

"I hear people talking in the parking lot."

"That may distract him long enough for us to bolt. There's a spot there where the light's brighter." He pointed to the left, just past the corner of the post-office building, where light banished the darkness, making a deeper section of the tree line visible. "Avoid it. Go right, where the shadows are. Hopefully he's distracted by those shoppers or he's still got eyes on our other hiding place, because there's about four feet where his angle is good enough to spot us just before we hit the trees."

Ashley nodded, refusing to think about those four feet. It looked like four hundred miles.

"You hit the tree line, you angle toward the road and go as hard as you can, even if it hurts. I'll be right behind you."

Ashley nodded again, not trusting her voice. Adrenaline had temporarily dulled the aches in her body, but there was no telling how long it would last. Ethan was right to angle toward the road. Anyone following would expect them to go for deeper cover in the woods, away from lights and traffic.

Ethan held up three fingers and counted down silently.

As soon as the last finger curled under, Ashley set everything inside on the broad oak and ran. If she could get to the tree, she'd be safe. One victory at a time.

She steeled her mind and her skin tensed like a sheet of iron, waiting for the strike of a bullet. When she hit the tree line, she dashed past her safe tree for one a few feet farther in, larger in diameter by at least a foot. She skidded on wet leaves and went down, scrambling up without missing a step before she slid around the tree and pressed her back against it, waiting for any sound indicating her position had been compromised.

When she heard nothing, she hazarded a peek, hands digging into the rough bark as she panted for air, expecting to see Ethan right behind her.

But he remained at the truck, weapon in hand, leaving Ashley alone in the woods.

TWELVE

Crouched behind the pitiful shelter of his truck tire, Ethan watched Ashley start for the trees, then turned his attention toward what he couldn't see: their attacker. He trained his ears on the parking lot next door where a car door slammed, driving up Ethan's itch to move. Either the shoppers Ashley had heard were merely getting into their vehicle or their friend had spotted her and was making no pretense of hiding.

He pivoted on his heel, gun resting against the side of his thigh, in time to see Ashley disappear into the trees. He'd wait thirty seconds then go, just to make certain no one followed. They were the thirty longest ticks of the clock he'd ever endured, his fingers so tight on his pistol he'd be shocked if indentations weren't permanently embedded in the grip when this was over.

When his mind tagged *thirty*, he didn't hesitate, just ran as hard as his crouched legs would carry him, the woods a million miles farther than he'd calculated in his head. He kept pushing, knowing Ashley was somewhere in front of him and he had to reach her.

"Ethan!"

The harsh whisper came from behind and to the left. He slid to a halt on the damp leaves and whipped around, forcing his weapon close to his side. If he aimed a gun at Ashley, she'd never forgive him.

She crouched low by a wide oak tree, half hidden in shadow.

And she'd never looked more beautiful than she did right then, relatively safe and unharmed.

He exhaled loudly and slipped to her position, making himself as small as possible behind a nearby tree, peering around it to try to make out the white sedan. It still sat in the parking lot, rear window partially open, but reflection blocked any view into the tinted window.

He allowed himself two seconds then turned his attention to Ashley. "We have to keep moving."

She nodded and the two of them stepped forward, farther from the post office, closer to the road, but far enough in the woods to avoid any headlights. They pushed ahead as quickly as they could until they reached the road across from the gas station they'd passed earlier.

"What now?" Ashley scanned left and right, likely seeing the same thing he did. The gas station flooded the road with light, making it too risky for them to cross. Hanging a left would keep them in darkness and take them in the direction of Fort Drum, but it also held a lot of variables.

Fort Drum, despite being close, was too far for them to hike. Besides, whom would he talk to when he got there? This Special Missions Unit was so secret, even the brass there wouldn't have a clue it existed, and they'd have every reason to doubt his word and deny him help.

But they couldn't stop moving. Ethan eyed a car sitting empty at a gas pump, engine running. What he wouldn't give to slip across the street and use it to make a quick getaway, but he'd never resorted to thievery, even in the name of a mission, and he wasn't about to start now.

Although with Ashley's safety on the line, it was a tempting prospect.

Ethan dug deep to several years ago when he'd been stationed at Drum with Ashley. Where exactly did this road go? The gunman was going to figure out any second now—if he hadn't already—they'd slipped away from him. It wouldn't be long before he and any cronies he'd called started combing the area.

He was on his own, and he'd never felt so helpless.

Except, he wasn't. *Lord, I need help. Some way out of this. For Ashley.*

No lightning bolt vaporized the threat. No thundering voice brought an idea. Just peace.

And the sound of Ashley fidgeting beside him. He needed to get her moving before she had time to over-think the situation, time to panic. They had to find a way to Sackets Harbor and Tate Walker's bed-and-breakfast.

That was it. The answer. He grabbed Ashley's wrist as he holstered his sidearm and reached for the phone in his pocket. He hid the light from the screen in his coat, tapped out a quick text then slipped the device into his hip pocket. Tate would come for them, but it would take close to an hour.

"Who'd you text?" Ashley watched him closely. "I thought you were alone now that..." She cleared her throat and shivered, but he had no idea whether it was from the cold or Mitchum's chilling death.

"An old friend." Having Tate seen with him could jeopardize everything the man meant to their unit, but no other way showed itself. They'd have to risk it. Ethan tipped his head toward a spot about a quarter mile up the road where darkness enveloped the area. "We'll cross there. If I'm remembering right, there are some outbuildings where we can hide."

Ashley asked no questions. Instead she slipped away from him. "I'll lead the way."

One waypoint at a time.

From pine tree to oak tree. Oak tree to larger oak tree. One small lifeline to another. She only had to live one second at a time.

Ashley pushed harder than she'd ever pushed in her life, every muscle in her body reminding her it had been less than twenty-four hours since she'd been bounced around inside her vehicle. Even her hair ached. But she kept going, Ethan urging her every step.

She chose her next target—a broad pine tree with a bend in the trunk—and kept moving.

A force behind her jerked her backward, smashing her against Ethan's chest and rattling her teeth together. Before she could comprehend the motion, she was on her knees, crouching beside Ethan in dense underbrush.

Her mind wanted to ask questions, but long-forgotten training kept her mute. Beside her, he eyed the road, then pointed back the way they'd come.

A car moved slowly up the road, a flashlight trained on the woods.

Ashley bit her lip as the white car passed, flashlight beam not strong enough to penetrate the darkness where they hid. She allowed herself a small sigh of relief before she realized the vehicle was headed straight for their destination. Reaching into her inside jacket pocket, she fingered the package containing Sean's lifeline, reassurance that this was worth it. But what now?

His mouth was a tight line as he watched the car's taillights disappear, but then he grinned. "I think he's on his own."

She read his lips more than she heard his whisper. "How do you know?"

The grin widened. "He's the only one looking. Not another soul has come this way searching. He left his post by the truck to seek us out. Unless this is a giant bluff, there's no one but him. That means they posted him as a guard and his backup isn't here yet."

"So we can get the truck?" *Please let it be so.* The pickup was her home base, her safe place. She'd grown dependent on that truck as a constant in her life.

That truck and the man beside her.

The lines on his face tightened. "No." He shook his head with a rueful smile. "Mitchum would get his finger in my face and tell me I deserved this for getting his truck riddled with bullet holes."

"But if they're not watching your vehicle—"

"I don't know for sure. It's off-limits unless we have to use it as a last resort." He chuckled low. "I just bought it."

Ashley didn't see the humor. She eased to a crouch and focused on the next tree, anxious to keep moving. Somehow she needed to find something besides Ethan to hold on to, because God kept ripping safety out from under her. God just kept proving what she'd learned years ago. He was a deity who couldn't be trusted.

Ethan's fingers encircled her biceps and held her still. "Wait for our guy to come back around. He's going to figure out we couldn't have gone very far." He tilted his head toward the lights from the gas station, reflecting dully on the damp road several yards away. "Hopefully, he'll stop to ask if anyone's seen us."

Nausea broke over Ashley in violent waves and she bit her lip to keep herself together. Ethan didn't understand. If she wasn't moving, fear would catch her. He'd already seen her panic once, and she didn't want to sit still long enough for him to see it again. Her fingers drummed a rapid beat on her thigh as she fidgeted. As much as she wanted to, she couldn't stop moving. Turning her eyes to the sky, she sought the stars, anything to count, to keep her mind from rocketing out of control and taking her body with it, but the trees and low cloud cover obscured her view.

She fidgeted, twisted, tried to find something to focus on, anything other than the dark road and lights that could come down at any minute and pinpoint them, anything other than every rustle of the trees that could indicate Ethan was wrong and someone was hot on their trail. This natural area wasn't very big. Even now, the barrel of a gun could be pointed right at her head.

Her fingers went numb. She was going to die here in the woods and, at the moment, she wasn't even sure if she cared anymore. At least the fear would be dead, too.

She rocked back and forth, her back bumping something solid as she did. She hesitated. Had Ethan been that close all along?

His arms slipped around her, pulling her tight against his chest, chasing away the chill as he rocked a different, slower beat than her frantic fidgeting. His breath was warm against her neck as he lowered his forehead to the back of her head, not saying a word, just rocking her.

Ashley held on to his forearms as though he anchored her to the planet. The rough fabric of his coat warmed her fingers, pink from too long in the cold without her gloves. She focused on the texture of the fabric, on his lips against her hair, on the security of his arms around her bringing silence into her raging thoughts.

Ethan was here. He was always where she needed him to be. He wasn't going to let anything happen to her.

Gradually the fear evaporated with her breath, barely visible in the damp night air.

Ethan didn't let her go. He could have at any time. But letting go was the last thing Ashley wanted. What she wanted was for Ethan to be the place she landed when she was afraid, the rock that wouldn't move in her upside-down world. After lying to herself since the day he'd walked out of her life, she knew she still loved him. The need to be near him grew with every second he comforted her with silent understanding.

With a sigh that puffed vapor into the air, Ashley let her muscles relax and settled against Ethan.

His muscles tightened reflexively, as though he was still on alert, watching for their pursuer to return. Or guarding himself against her.

As he should be. Now, in these woods, being pursued by a man with a gun, was not the time to be thinking these thoughts. Emotions such as these could get her killed. She straightened as she turned, intent on telling Ethan she was fine now, thanks for understanding.

But his head was still inches from hers and her eyes caught his off guard.

They locked and his softened, every line falling away, every bit of vigilance disappearing into something completely different, something Ashley fell into and never wanted to climb out of.

Ethan had been about to pull away when Ashley turned, his feelings with her in his arms completely out of step with the situation they were in. But heightened adrenaline and grief and something about Ashley needing him, leaning against him, fully trusting him for the first time, undid his rational thinking. She was too close. He dropped his forehead to hers, tugging her near. If he wanted, he could close those last inches and start something entirely new between them.

If he did, it was entirely possible neither of them would live to see the morning, because getting lost in her would leave them wide open to anyone who might sneak up on them.

And it would leave his heart wide open to what he couldn't have.

Deliberately, he pulled his arms away, drew his head back and set her at a distance, even though doing so felt as if she was attached to his heart and ripping it from his body with every inch. Denying her a second time in one day would probably cost him her love forever.

Which was the way it should be.

But he still couldn't let her think he was pushing her away because she meant nothing. He stood and took a step back, watching the road. "I have to pay attention, stay focused if we're going to get out of here." He held out a hand to her, unable to shove her away completely.

She turned away and he fought the muscles in his arm that twitched to reach out and pull her close again, defying common sense. If he kissed her it would be acknowledging he loved her, and it would violate Sean's claim to her.

But if Sean was the one she cared for, why was she looking at him that way? He opened his mouth to say her name, to ask her if all his assumptions were wrong, but clamped it shut as headlights came toward them, the flashlight still playing along the road. He found her wrist and pulled her lower, praying the dense underbrush would keep them hidden for one more pass.

They needed to get going. By his calculations, they had forty-five minutes to stay hidden and still cover the half mile to the rendezvous point with Tate. A monumental task.

As the sedan came closer, Ashley stiffened, though she didn't huddle close to him as she had before. Likely she never would again, but there wasn't time to think of that as the beam of the flashlight bounced just feet in front of them. *Please, God. Please let him stop at the store and give us the chance to move.*

As if the shooter heard Ethan's prayer, he killed the flashlight and sped up to pull into the parking lot of the gas station, where he slid in beside a four-wheel-drive SUV. Ethan edged up to watch as the man, stocky and dark, climbed out to consult with the driver of the SUV, pointing toward the post office, then up the road to where they hid.

Wait. This was backup. Which meant...

"Ashley, we have to move. Now."

"What?"

His smile was grim. "We have to risk going to the truck." He pointed to the gas station as he pulled her to stand. "Those are the guys he's called, and they'll be on foot in these woods before we can get to where Tate's meeting us. We've got to gamble they left the truck without someone watching it or we'll never get out of here."

"But you said..." Her voice trailed off in a question he couldn't answer.

He was well aware of what he'd said, but instinct whispered there was no other choice. If he let those guys get on foot and start looking, giving the driver time to return to the post office, they were dead. The truck was their one shot at freedom.

He hauled her the rest of the way to her feet. "Can you run this one more time?"

She rolled her eyes, bitterness hardening her features. "What choice do I have?"

He knew she was tired of repeating the words, knew the helplessness eating at her every time she said them. Only this time she didn't realize how right she was.

One last glance at the men in the parking lot revealed four climbing from the truck wearing coats much too heavy for the light spring chill. He shuddered to think what hid underneath. "Go."

Ashley must have heard the urgency, because she shot forward like a rabbit, running faster than she'd come in. Ethan stayed close on her heels, branches slapping at his skin, one slashing across his cheekbone with a razor's bite. Warm blood trickled down his face.

At the edge of the woods Ashley dropped to a crouch and Ethan landed right beside her, partially blocking her from whatever lay on the other side.

Nothing moved in the post-office parking lot and, as far as he could see, there were no cars in the lot of the store next door. It was too quiet, too easy.

But the vision of those men prepared to stalk into the woods drove him forward. They were between the proverbial rock and a hard place, and the truck was their only means of escape. They probably had less than a minute before the white sedan or the SUV came to stand guard, and Ethan had no doubt the firepower in the SUV would be more than enough to do the job they'd come to do. To kill him and steal Ashley.

Ethan pulled his key fob from his pocket, finger poised on the unlock button for the truck. As before, he held up three fingers, gave the area a final sweep and counted down to run. This time he didn't send Ashley alone. They burst from the woods together as bullets flew right behind them, Ethan pressing the unlock button in time for Ashley to dive in through the passenger door.

Ethan skidded around the vehicle and stumbled to a halt.

A man was crouched near the back tire, a pistol equipped with a silencer taking dead aim at Ethan's head.

He deflated as the man smiled, squaring his aim.

There would be no dialogue, just the shot that killed him. Well, he'd go down fighting. His muscles tightened into knots as he prepared to dive straight toward the man who could end his life and take Ashley away from him.

Before he could move, the back door of the truck flew open and crashed against the man's arm, sending the gun skittering across the pavement.

Ethan flicked a quick glance to see Ashley duck back into the truck as the stunned gunman staggered to his feet. Ethan didn't give him the chance. He launched himself at the truck door, swinging it shut with the entire force of his body, capturing his assailant's arm and shoulder in the door with a thick crunch.

The man threw back his head and roared in pain.

With an uppercut, Ethan slammed the man's mouth shut, driving his head back and dropping him to the ground. He lay there, stunned, cradling his injured arm as he tried to roll onto his side.

Ethan didn't wait for him to get up. Instead he yanked the driver's door open and shoved the key in the ignition before he settled in. "Put your seat belt on. You're going to need it."

He checked the side mirror, then yanked the truck into Reverse and to the left to avoid the man who'd staggered to his knees, clutching his injured shoulder.

Ethan meant to be out of range before he raised an alarm. Tires squealing, he threw the truck out of the parking lot and up the road, praying they had a jump on the white sedan and the dark SUV.

Rather than take the direct route to the highway, he spun a right onto 342 and thanked God again for the time he'd been stationed at Drum. Let them think he was headed toward the post. As long as no one picked up on his intent to get to Sackets Harbor and Tate's B and B, they'd be safe.

He alternated between watching the road behind him and the road in front of him, while Ashley rode silently, clutching the package from Sean with both hands.

In the distance, a car fell in behind them, but it didn't seem to be in a hurry. Ethan took the first left he could find and coached his leg muscles to ease up on the gas pedal, waiting to see if the car followed.

It didn't. He allowed himself to relax for the first time since the shot fired twenty minutes ago. Unless he was wrong about everything, they'd managed to get away. He abandoned the mirrors and appraised Ashley.

With trembling fingers, she brushed long blond strands from her eyelashes and wrapped her hands around the envelope again. In spite of everything, including the white of her knuckles, she seemed to be holding on. Maybe there was a limit to even what her panic could do in one day. Her body had to run out of adrenaline at some point, didn't it?

He wanted to reach for her, but there wasn't a lot of wisdom in that. "You got this?"

Her eyes scanned the road, the glove box and finally her feet. She stretched her stiff fingers toward the heat vent before she answered, a tremble beginning at her fingertips and rattling her entire body. "Fine. Just cold. From the inside out."

"Your adrenaline's ebbing." Ethan turned up the heat

and tried to gauge their location. "Give it a few minutes. You'll warm up." He cleared his throat. "Quick thinking with the door."

"When you didn't get in the car, I knew I needed to do something. Did he have...?"

She couldn't even say the word, and it was probably a good thing she hadn't seen it. He certainly wasn't going to tell her. "Weapon or not, you took him down and gave me the out we needed. I'd have been proud to have you on my team."

"Well, there's something that'll never happen." She crossed her arms over her chest, cutting off any further conversation.

He'd said the wrong thing. Done all of the wrong things. If he wasn't careful, she'd shut down and walk away before they solved this thing...and before his feelings grew any stronger.

THIRTEEN

Ashley sank to the edge of the sofa and ran her hands along the multicolored upholstery, the fabric rough under her fingers. In other circumstances, the small bed-and-breakfast could have been a haven for her. The alcove at the top of the stairs held a small, modern sofa and a recliner, as well as a full bookcase standing sentry by a set of French doors leading out to a small balcony. The deep purple of the walls and the heavy lace curtains at the windows reached in and soothed something deep inside her. If she closed her eyes, she could imagine the harbor calling to her from just down the street.

Tate Walker and his ex-wife had chosen an ideal location for their B and B in Sackets Harbor, a place Ashley could find peace in a different situation.

For now she reveled in a few minutes of solitude after a few hours of sleep and a hot shower. She'd argued with Ethan about sleeping, knowing every moment counted, but even she couldn't deny her mind needed refreshing for the job ahead.

She couldn't sit here much longer. With Sean's data in hand, she had work to do deciphering the code so Ethan could pass along vital intel. Every hour was valuable.

From the living room downstairs, Ethan's words drifted,

mingling with another muffled voice, though the conversation was too far away to decipher. The low drone of the TV overlaid the men's discussion. Ashley closed her eyes again and let Ethan's deep timbre wash over her, let herself get comfortable.

Too comfortable. The instant she thought she'd found a place to hold on to, God snatched it away.

Her apartment.

The cabin.

Ethan's truck—a home base for her throughout these past twenty-four hours. Now easily identifiable, it had to be ditched.

Tate had met them at a park-and-ride lot on north 81 near the Canadian border before they'd wound their way to Sackets Harbor, the trip taking much too long for Ashley's taste. She'd ridden nausea the whole way, unable to stop watching out the window, even after Ethan and Tate had both assured her they weren't being followed.

A small crash took her to the window, muscles trembling. *Please, God. Not again.*

In the backyard, early morning sunlight cast a soft glow across the lawn. Tate walked out of a wooden shed at the back of the property, surveyed his small yard, then dragged a manual push mower out and started to mow grass that, this early in the season, really didn't need attention.

Tate Walker was exactly what Ashley pictured a friend of Ethan's to be. Tall and muscular, in his late thirties, Tate's black hair was already sprinkled with salt, his green eyes lined with military experience. His ready smile, even in the midst of chaos, had made Ashley relax and almost feel at home.

A creak on the stairs pulled her from the window and

highlighted the silence in the house, the TV downstairs conspicuously mute.

Ethan leaned against the stair rail. The dark green of his sweater dragged the brown from his eyes and deepened the color to hot chocolate. Beneath his right eye, a cut marred his skin—a souvenir from their mad dash through the woods. He'd been watching her, and she had no idea how long.

When he realized he had her attention, he nodded, a grim look tightening the lines around his mouth. "You all right up here?"

Better now that he was here, though there was no way she'd ever say those words out loud. He might not be the self-centered man she'd believed him to be, but once this job was finished, he'd be on to his next mission. Another safe place gone. No matter how much she wanted to go to him now and let him hold her, she couldn't. It would only hurt more later.

Still…something was wrong. It was written in the lines around his eyes. He was about to tell her they needed to run again.

She was tired. So tired. She'd dozed for a few hours in one of the guest rooms, but the first light of dawn had dragged her to consciousness again. The sleep wasn't enough to compensate for two days' worth of adrenaline and fear. She needed a safe place to lay her head for more than a few hours before they needed to find transportation and hit the road again.

She steeled herself, already reaching for the bag that held her newly purchased laptop and her one change of clothes. "Where to now?"

Ethan shook his head with a rueful smile. "Nowhere. At least not for a little while. Where we ditched the truck, they're going to think we headed for Canada. And they'd have to dig pretty deep to find any way of connecting me to Tate and this place. The time we served together was…classified."

Classified. Secret. Like so much else about him.

"Then what's wrong?"

He shook his head and crossed his arms over his chest, though he still tried to look as though his leaning against the stairwell was supposed to be a casual thing. The tightness in his fingers on his biceps gave him away. "You know, Colson, it's a good thing the bad guys can't read me as well as you do. I'd never be able to go undercover again."

"You're easy to read." She waved a hand, gesturing up and down his height. "Everything about you gives you away."

"Only to you." The words were low, almost gravelly with regret.

She couldn't look at him anymore. Knowing him that well was only going to make goodbye harder. "You haven't told me what's wrong."

"Because I really, really don't want to."

Ashley's bones melted, bile rising in her throat. Tears beat against the backs of her eyelids as she sank to the couch. Sean. He had news about Sean, and from the sound of his voice, it wasn't good.

"Ethan. Is Sean…?" She couldn't even bring herself to say the word.

He was at her side, settled on the edge of the sofa, his shoulder leaning against hers. He didn't put his arm around her, though she sure wished he would. "No. Sean's status hasn't changed as far as I know. I've got Tate working on it. He's part of the old-school network I was telling you about, and I'm hoping he can get some answers, though it might not be quick. I have to believe, though, that

Sean's okay." He dragged a hand down his uninjured cheek and along his chin, the stubble scraping harshly. "They won't do anything to him until they know how much he was able to pass this way and, so far, we still have that information with us." He leaned his shoulder heavier against hers and reached for her hand. "There's something else."

It wasn't possible for her to sink lower, but she did, even as her heart twinged at the warmth of his fingers around hers. "Tell me before my imagination paints a worse picture than you're about to lie out there."

"I don't know how…but they tracked us to your grandparents' cabin." Ethan squeezed her fingers. "It's been burned. There's nothing left."

Ashley's breath caught in her throat. Her grandparents' pride and joy, the site of her happiest moments from childhood…gone. "Katrina?"

"I don't know anything official."

Needing to move, to pace, to do anything other than sit still, Ashley pushed herself up, pulling her hand from Ethan's. She crossed to the French doors and started to step out but thought better of it. In the light of day, anyone could see her. Instead, she leaned her head against the white paint of the frame. "How do you know all of this? You don't know anything about Sean, but you know my family's cabin is gone?" Anger bubbled in her. At Ethan, at Sean, at the men who were intent on wrecking every part of her life all to keep their revenue stream flowing.

Money. It all boiled down to money.

The sofa squeaked as Ethan turned to face her. "While you were in the shower this morning, I had Tate turn on the news. I needed to see how many headlines a shooting at the airport and a dead soldier are generating. Turns out, not too many. They attributed the airport shooting to gang violence, and there hasn't been a mention about

Mitchum yet. But there was a story about a cabin burning farther upstate on the river and I recognized the structure. It made the news because they were afraid it would get out of control and spread to the woods."

"And Katrina?"

There was another creak and then Ethan's hands were on her shoulders, his forehead against the back of her head, just like in the woods. "On the news video, her car was still in the driveway. And the reporter said they'd—"

"Found a body." Ashley pressed her hands to her mouth and tipped her head forward, squeezing her eyes shut as the tears forced their way out. What had they done? It had been her idea to hide at the cabin. It was her fault her cousin was dead. Somehow, she'd led the people who wanted to kill her straight to her family. There was no reason to murder Katrina, no reason to burn the cabin other than to send a message to Ethan and her. A message that said they'd better give up before they were caught.

A message that said they couldn't win.

Ashley crumbled in front of his eyes. She buried her face in her hands, great sobs heaving her shoulders, choking her.

The sound cracked every last carefully constructed wall around Ethan's heart. He wanted to walk out the front door and face these guys head-on, bare-fisted if it took that, just to free Ashley from this pain. As gently as he could, he turned her to face him and pulled her close, determined to shelter her from the world even if it was for only a few minutes. He held her tight, protecting her the way he should have when she'd needed him most.

"I've led these guys right to my family." He heard Ashley's muffled words against his chest as her sobs slowed. "What if Sean's already—?"

Ethan didn't give her time to finish the sentence. He pushed her gently away, planting his hands on her shoulders. He wanted to keep holding her, but he couldn't let her believe the lie. "No. This is not your fault. None of this is your fault. This is the fault of power-hungry, bloodthirsty men who will stop at nothing to destroy our way of life and everything we stand for. If anything, Sean and I are to blame for getting you involved in the first place. We pointed those guys right to you, and I'm sorry. I'm sorrier than you know. You have to believe me." He ran a hand down her hair, fingers tracing across her cheek, trying to telegraph his conviction to her, to let her know the weight of everything about this situation rested squarely on his shoulders, and he was going to make it right. "Look at me."

She swallowed hard and lifted her head, eyes meeting his. The intensity of that green blew away everything he'd planned to say, every argument he'd prepared. Instead what he saw there brought the rush of every emotion he'd experienced since he'd jerked her into his life. Grief, triumph, fear...love. The onslaught tore down his last defenses. He scanned her eyes, seeing it all reflected at him. They were caught in this together, always had been.

His gaze drifted to her hair, to the window behind her, back to her eyes. He let his thumb shift to the side of her neck, where he brushed her hair aside, the soft skin warming his thumb and melting his fortitude. "The only thing that matters to me is you. And right now you're safe." Safe from the terrorists...but probably not safe from him.

He brushed a kiss across her forehead, and when she leaned in, he was finished. He knew he shouldn't do this. She was an asset to protect, one whose presence tended to tear apart all of his training. And still, always, Sean was between them. He eased her away. As much as he didn't want to, he had to step out of the warmth of her presence.

Backing toward the stairs, he shook his head. "I can't. I have to protect you and I can't if we…" He exhaled loudly, changing tactics. "You and Sean belong together. He's the one who deserves you."

Ashley's eyebrows pulled together, grief overtaken by confusion. "That makes no sense. Sean is a friend. Our getting engaged was a huge mistake. I love him, but he's like my brother." She tossed a hand in the air in frustration, voice ragged with emotion. "It's you, Ethan. It's always been you."

There was no more to be said. Ethan closed the space between them in two steps, pulling her toward him and pressing his lips to hers in a kiss almost a decade in the making, pouring everything he felt into her, from the fear he'd experienced the day she was shot to the grief over the happenings of the past two days, to his fierce desire to make sure nothing ever hurt her again…not even him.

She met him halfway, receiving everything he gave.

His fingers tangled in her hair, pulling her closer as he dived into the moment he never thought he'd have.

But then she broke the kiss, backing away from him and laying her hands against his chest, though she didn't leave his embrace. She wouldn't meet his eyes, just stood there as his arms slipped around her back and his heartbeat pounded against her palms.

She pulled in a ragged breath, let it out, then shuddered another one, tears pooling in her eyes and running down her cheeks. Finally she shook her head and pressed tighter against his chest, pushing him away.

"We can't do this." She sidestepped him and walked to the chair in the corner of the room, lifting her laptop with trembling fingers.

"What?" He hated the word. It sounded feeble and pleading. Everything he wasn't supposed to be. But he'd just held everything in his arms and it was gone. Far from wrecking his focus, this moment solidified his desire to protect her to the end, and now she was separating them. How he sounded was irrelevant.

She wrapped her arms around the laptop and pressed it to her chest. "Because, Ethan. I can't lose you." She rolled her eyes to the ceiling, wiped at a tear and looked somewhere over his head. "Because every single safe place I have, God takes away. My parents, my future, my home, my cousin... And you?" She sniffed and swallowed hard, choking on the next words. "You're the safest place of all. I can't risk you. It would kill me."

He stepped toward her. "I'm not going anywhere." Not now that he knew the truth, that her feelings ran as deeply as his.

"You can't make that promise." The tears vanished, swallowed by a voice so hard it should have physically pained him. She shook her head, eyes glittering. "You can't. Because you'll be gone just as soon as there's another mission. And if you don't leave, then God will take you by some other means, because my life works that way."

Ethan forgot everything he was thinking in the face of her raw pain. This wasn't about him. It was about something so much bigger. It was fear and faith and the blueprint of her entire life.

"God doesn't operate like that."

"Maybe not in your life. And since when do you care?"

"Since the day you nearly died in front of me and He saved you." The back of Ethan's neck ached and he dug his fingers into muscles that refused to yield. He'd just found her, and if he couldn't make her understand, he would lose her. "I never thought I needed God until then, but when I was about to lose everything I cared about, He's where I ran. When the smoke cleared and everything died down and I got time to think, I realized that. At my lowest, I knew what was real. Something in me knew where to call. And do you know where I learned it?"

He took another step toward her, desperate to reach her. "You. You and your faith from the day we first met. Even with your parents dying and all you and Sean went through, you both held on to Jesus. You knew He cared even when it seemed like everything in the world was against you."

She froze, fingers pressing the laptop against her chest so tightly her knuckles whitened. Her nose twitched, but then her lips pressed even tighter together and she shook her head again. "Well, I was wrong. We were both wrong." She turned away from him and marched for the stairs. "We need to go downstairs and work on decoding Sean's files, because nobody's going to save him but the two of us." Without looking back, she disappeared from view before firing a parting shot. "We're running out of time."

FOURTEEN

Ashley looked up from the laptop screen as a cup of coffee appeared on the table at her right hand.

Tate slid into the seat across from her with his own steaming mug. "You look like you have a long night ahead of you. Thought you might need it." He'd appeared periodically throughout the day, offering food, puttering around and generally pretending he wasn't standing guard while Ethan caught some much-needed sleep.

Ashley tilted her head from one side to the other, stretching muscles tight from hunching over a computer rewriting code for hours and from the pounding memory of Ethan's kiss. Its constant replay in her mind made the work that should have taken a handful of hours drag on for the entire day. Constantly looking up to see if he was entering the room had taken up another chunk of time she didn't care to add up. He hadn't appeared since she'd walked out on him.

Why should he? She'd shoved him away and told him she wanted nothing to do with him. She'd had everything she'd ever wanted holding her in his arms, and fear had wrecked it just like everything else in her life.

It was for the best. Better to watch him walk away now

than to completely lose herself to him and be destroyed when he was gone.

The faster she decoded Sean's information, the faster she could get Ethan out of her life for good.

Before God took him away.

Control. This time, she was in the driver's seat and she got to say when something left her life.

"Thanks. Probably going to be another all-nighter for me." She reached for the heavy, white coffee mug and cradled it in her hands, the warmth easing a little bit of the chill in her bones. A few minutes of not thinking would be nice. "Were you outside mowing the grass this morning? Before it's even had a chance to grow?"

"Helps me think. Seems like you and Ethan brought me a lot to ponder. So what if the neighbors assume I've lost my marbles?" Tate smiled and took a sip of his coffee then set his mug on the table and twisted it back and forth, one finger on the handle, eyes on the motion of the coffee inside. "So, you're Sean Turner's ex-fiancée."

Ashley sat back harder in the chair and kept her mouth shut. He shouldn't know that.

Tate glanced up, seemed to read her expression and straightened. "It's okay. Really." He had the good sense to look a bit sheepish. "I guessed. Ethan didn't tell me. Sean and I worked pretty closely together in the past, and I knew he'd been engaged to a girl who was more sister than wife material. And Ethan has talked so much about you…" He cleared his throat and shut his mouth, looking as though he wished he could take back his last few words.

She'd let him. The last thing Ashley wanted to talk about was Ethan, even though the woman in her was dying to know what he had said to the man across from her. "So you know him?"

"Sean? Yeah." Tate settled against the long wooden

bench running under the window on the other side of the table, relaxing at her change of subject. "When Sean first discovered there was a problem, I was the closest operator to him, so I was first contact. We talked a lot. Worked together a bit before I medically retired."

He had her interest. Sliding the laptop to the side, Ashley sat forward, elbows on the table. "You medically retired? Why?"

Tate looked to the ceiling, his posture going rigid.

Guilt welled from her toes to her throat. "I'm sorry. I…I don't like to talk about it, either."

"Don't be sorry. It's a pretty recent thing, a crazy couple of years I'm still getting over." Tate met her gaze with his green eyes, then rested a hand on his chest and tapped it with an index finger. "What happened when you were shot? According to Ethan, you'd have made a crackerjack team leader."

Ashley traced the edge of the laptop with her index finger. She'd never talked to anyone about that day, had let the few people close to her settle for their own experiences. But sitting with Tate after all that had happened, the need to unburden herself was too much.

"I was shot on a domestic-violence call." Her hand drifted to the scar. There it was, the core reason she'd never been able to recover, the reason she was afraid. She'd held all of the control wielding her weapon, but it hadn't been enough. If she couldn't control that situation, she couldn't control anything. She cleared her throat, unwilling to sink into those thoughts. "It was close-range to the side of my abdomen and recovery was long. Right when it was all getting better, I got hit with an infection that nearly took me out all over again." The fear had moved in, had sent her running when it became clear reenlistment was not an option. She'd lost control facing an assailant, and then she'd been felled by her own body. She traced the pattern on the cover of the laptop. There was everything to fear in a world where nothing was in her control. Everything.

If she continued to let herself remember, to focus on the situation at hand, she'd never finish the mission Sean and Ethan had dragged her into. Edging the laptop another inch away, she turned the spotlight on the man across the table. "What about you?" The question was blunt, but the air between them spoke of shared pain and loss, bonded them in a way Ashley hadn't felt with anyone else.

"A lot of it is classified, but…" Tate traced a scar in the table. "I was on a long-term assignment when I met Sean. Involved a group manipulating shipping manifests to funnel drugs into the country from Afghanistan. One of the grunts figured out I was undercover. Still don't know how, but it's possible there's a link to the mole that's wreaking havoc on this investigation, too."

Tate took a long sip of coffee and grimaced at the heat. "I had my gun, but we were hand-to-hand. He had a knife. A big one. And, long story short, you can live with just one lung, even if you can't do your dream job anymore. They offered me medical retirement and I took it…at least on paper."

Ashley pulled the corner of her lip between her teeth. Tate had lost control of his own situation, yet here he sat, talking about it as if he was okay with the outcome even though he'd had his life, his dream, derailed, too. "And are you happy here? Running a bed-and-breakfast? After working with Ethan and investigating and the… adrenaline?"

The adrenaline. It used to be her best friend, the thing that let her know she was alive after her parents died. Now all it did was wreck her fear.

Tate chuckled, smile lines framing his eyes. "I'm a piece in a bigger puzzle, Ashley. We all are. Only one who can see the whole puzzle is God. I can think I fit one place, but somewhere on the other side of the board, there's another better place, where I was made to be. God's got a way of moving you where He needs you."

"So God made that guy stab you." Sounded about right, considering what He'd done to her.

"No, and he didn't make my wife leave me, either." Tate leaned closer, trapping her in his gaze. "You hear me when I say this. God doesn't cause bad things to happen to you. He didn't cause you to get shot and He didn't cause me to get stabbed, but He'll use it when it happens." He sat back and crossed his arms. "But you have to get out of the way and let Him. It took me a long time to get over being angry with Him, and when I did, He showed me a whole new thing."

Ashley didn't want a whole new thing. She wanted her old dream, wanted to do what Tate had done, what Ethan and Sean were doing. As Ethan had said, this job was made for her. But she wasn't about to whine to Tate Walker about her problems. The man had lost a lung. "How did you know I was shot?"

"Because I've known Ethan Kincaid a long time. And I know his life changed that day." Tate ran his tongue along his top teeth. "Ashley, you have to let go of the idea that there's only one thing in life for you. And you have to let go of the lie that God's got it out for you."

"But your dream, everything you trained for…"

Tate chuckled low. "Dreams change. Remember, I said I retired on paper. Things aren't always what they seem."

"No, they're not." Ethan's voice entered the room from behind her.

Ashley whipped around, sloshing hot coffee on her

hand. She'd almost—almost—forgotten he was in the house. "Where've you been?" She couldn't swallow the question fast enough. The last thing she needed was for him to know she'd noticed his absence.

He let his eyes linger on her for a moment before he looked over her head at Tate. "It worked."

"You got what you needed?"

"You're a lifesaver, man."

Tate grinned. "That's what I do." He stood and pointed to the coffeemaker. "Made Ashley a pot, but there's some soda in the fridge if you need a caffeine fix. I'll clear out now and let you do what you've got to do. Wake me if you need me. And feel free to fill in your friend on what's going on here." He winked at Ashley. "Think about what I said."

She'd fallen down the rabbit hole. She was sure of it. These two made about as much sense as the Mad Hatter and his picnic table full of guests.

Ethan grabbed a can of soda, then slipped into the spot Tate had vacated, directly across from Ashley. Sliding Tate's still-steaming cup out of the way with a grimace, he gave her a slight smile, the amusement tweaking the scar at the corner of his right eye. "I heard you and Tate talking. You ought to see his office. Plaques from all over. If there was a school, he went to it. A combat theater, he was there. An award, he's got it. A guy like him would never be happy running a little old bed-and-breakfast in a small tourist town."

So, Ethan was going to play it that way, as though nothing had happened and she hadn't stalked out on him after he kissed her? Fine. She would never admit to him she was relieved. "So he teaches skydiving on the side? Climbs buildings dressed as Spider-Man? What?"

"Remember how I told you we do things 'old school,'

even though this unit is one of the most technologically advanced in the world?"

Ashley nodded slowly. "Because you know how to use the technology, you know the tech can be used against you."

"Bugs, tracers, viruses… Phones can be hacked. Lines can be tapped. Email can be traced. So we took a cue from our Revolutionary War brothers in arms."

"From the spy rings." In spite of everything, she was impressed. "One hands off to another and to another until the message reaches its intended recipient."

"Exactly. Like spoofing an email address around the world but in a low-tech way. Tate's one of those links in the chain. The B and B is a cover, because no one thinks it odd if a lot of people come and go. It's not a safe house, because there are often guests here, which makes it too risky. It's a communications center. Tate has the ability to pass information up the chain to get answers. Last night while you were sleeping, he ran a few things up for me. The guys chasing you can try, but it's going to take them some time to trace that combination of email, texts, landlines and internet messages."

Ashley leaned forward. "So you were able to get word about Sean?"

"Yes." Ethan wrapped his fingers around the soda can. "But you understand this is all quick doses of information that can be passed on quickly. It's not an in-depth report."

Ashley nodded, wanting to speed him up, to reach into his mind and get the information instead of waiting for him to vocalize it.

"He's alive."

Ashley sank against the chair. "What else?"

"Not much. We know the location where an interpreter last spotted him and they have some scouts looking. It's not a full-scale manhunt because it would attract too much attention and, frankly, if they get tipped off we're close, they'll lighten the load so they can save their own hides."

By killing Sean.

"I wish I had more for you, but that's all there is."

She pressed her thumb against her index finger, wishing he'd reach across the table and take her hand, connect with her, but she'd thrown that opportunity back at him. Necessarily so. "Is the cavalry coming for us?"

"No."

Ashley shoved her coffee cup to the side, anger surging. "No? But I thought—"

"Even over our network, I can't risk giving away our location because it would rat out us and Tate, too. I opened up the pipeline to find out how Sean is and to pass word about Mitchum. I can't risk opening it again. And we can't risk this whole operation by handing out our location and having a team come to us. You have to remember, someone is watching everything we do. Someone compromised Sean and, before him, Jacob. And someone compromised the safe house. Backup is out of the question."

It was too much. Ethan's kiss. Tate's words. No hope for rescue unless she stepped up... Her head swam, too much information trying to squeeze into too many narrow spaces.

Ethan exhaled loudly. "Ashley—" he slid her computer closer to her "—if you want this to be over, then let's finish this thing. Figure out what Sean's got, we'll find him, and we'll shut these guys down for good."

Ashley didn't move. Her hair fell forward, shielding her face from Ethan's view. He watched her, waiting. What he wanted was for her to up and tell him she saw the problem with her thinking. She'd thought this all through and she trusted God, could live with Ethan's life, with his job...with him.

But that wasn't going to happen. Instead, just when he was convinced she'd passed out from exhaustion, she lifted her head and wiped her hair out of her eyes. "Let's do this." She slid the chair beside her out with her foot. "You can come around and watch. Might be something you can work out with Sean later and use, though I'm guessing we'll hit a few bugs and I might have to rewrite more code."

Ethan slipped around the table, bringing his drink with him, and slid into the chair to her right.

She turned the screen toward him and pointed to a series of code running down the window. "I've been working the program all day, fixing some bugs I knew were there but never bothered with because when was I ever going to use this?"

"Tell me what it does exactly."

"We'd talked about it for a long time, but when I was recovering, we started to work on it. Kept me from watching too many TV movies and gave me something to focus on. Long story short, it's an encryption method." Ashley shut the code window and reached for the envelope beside her, dumping its contents onto the table. "These drives are encoded on Sean's end, and I should be able to decode them here, if I can figure out his cipher. I already checked the envelope and the exterior of the drives. There's nothing there. You're sure he didn't give you any clue?"

"None other than you'd know when you saw it."

"Well, I can't risk logging in to my email to see if he sent something there, but nothing comes to mind and I don't see anything here." Popping a drive into the USB slot, Ashley double clicked an icon.

Ethan leaned closer as another window opened, the

screen filling with thumbnails of photos. "Pictures. He didn't encrypt anything. These are surveillance photos."

Ashley opened several pictures, intent on the screen in front of her. "I think he…" She opened three more photos then laughed—the first time he'd heard the sound in years. Time stopped and everything else receded as Ethan took in the amusement on her face, the joy there for a brief second before she realized he was looking and stopped, though a smile still pulled at her lips.

"You're supposed to think they're surveillance photos." Ashley opened several more files and spread them across the screen. "If you found this and knew it was supposed to be Intelligence, what would you do?"

Ethan turned the screen toward him. A camel dominated the first shot, turned toward the camera, a brightly covered blanket thrown over its hump. Nothing suspicious immediately appeared. "I'd analyze the photos, look to see who they were surveilling, what they'd found out, what they know. Are there words, pictures, artifacts, dates, people…?"

"Precisely. You'd never know the picture is encrypted code hiding another file." Minimizing the screen, Ashley clicked on the camel photo file and dragged it to an icon on the screen, then typed something quickly. "I know what Sean's cipher is, and if I coded everything correctly…" A new file popped up and Ashley double clicked it to reveal a Department of Defense form.

"Steganography. Data hidden inside other data. There are some well-known instances of terrorists using it."

"Yes, but this is on a different level. Steeper encryption, less chance of file degradation, less chance of recognizing something like bit substitution. No matter how hard someone looks, they shouldn't be able to find the encryption."

"And you've been keeping this to yourself?"

"It's not ready. I'm just praying we can open half of what Sean's sent."

"I'm praying for a bigger percentage than half." He pulled the laptop from her reach and enlarged the document. "It's a DD-1149, used for shipping materials between Department of Defense sites. This one is particular to a handful of places, including New Cumberland. Tate was wounded there."

Ethan scratched his head, dragged his hand across his mouth and pointed at the screen, the excitement of a mission about to come together tingling in his gut. "Something tells me Sean's onto something huge here, even bigger than we thought. There may be links to several different terror cells on here. How many files are there?"

Ashley shrugged. "A couple hundred on this drive alone. I haven't checked the others." She decrypted five more files and revealed more DOD forms along with two emails.

Ethan whistled low. "No wonder they want these. If this is what I think it is, Sean's sent everything we need to sweep up the entire operation and bury it. What was the cipher?"

"Unfortunately it's not that simple. From the looks of it, Sean's been working on this for months. Each of these hundreds of files has its own key, its own unlock code embedded in the picture itself. If anyone finds the program and the files, they have to individually decode the encryption that unlocks each photo. It could take them years."

"And they can't just destroy the files, because they don't know if we have copies. Getting these drives is the only way they can figure out if we have enough to take them down and go on the defensive." Ethan sat back and eyed Ashley. "What are the keys?"

"They're all personal." She clicked to the original camel photo. "When I was a kid, I had a stuffed camel I got at the zoo in Washington. His name was Clyde."

"Clyde the Camel." Ethan snorted. "Like the old song by Ray Stevens?"

"My dad loved him. If you're going to laugh, I'll stop talking."

Ethan held up both hands in surrender.

"Anyway, Sean's family was with us. So it could be Clyde, Washington, Stevens, zoo… I have to figure out what he's trying to say by the main subject of the picture."

Ethan's smile faded. "So when Sean said you had the key, he meant you *are* the key. The only key." Ethan stood so fast the chair nearly toppled. He paced to the door and stared into the darkness out the small window.

Ashley slid away from the table. "Ethan?"

"This is bigger than I thought. You're not leverage against Sean." He came back to her, mind spinning. "They won't kill Sean until they know for sure they've wiped out every other avenue of decoding his information. They need him for his knowledge, to tell them everything we have on them and every piece of the operation. An operative in hand is gold to them. But you? You're the only person in the world who can decode what he's sent, what's physically in our hands. We can't hand this off to someone at headquarters and let them do it. It has to be you. Ash, their plan was never to take you. The plan all along has been to let you lead them to the drives and then to kill you."

FIFTEEN

"What I hear you saying is you need me to keep working." Ashley clicked another photo and studied it. A pickup. Toyota. Same brand Sean's grandfather had sold him right after he got his license. Her fingers tapped the keys. Grampy. Leo.

Ethan laid a hand on hers across the keyboard. "Ashley. Stop."

She shook her hand free and focused on the screen, trying to keep Ethan's words from penetrating her mind.

Carruthers. The file opened, revealing another email. She slid it to the side and clicked on the next photo.

"Ashley." This time Ethan slid the laptop out of reach, dropping her fingers to the table.

She stared at the screen. A dog. A gray dog. Sean owned a gray dog once. Misty. She reached for the computer, but Ethan slid it farther away.

"Stop. Listen." Ethan sank into his chair and turned her to face him, though she fought his attention. "I have to get you out of here, to Virginia, where we're headquartered." He reached for her hands. "This is more than you passing on one big piece of information. You're the big piece of information. It's going to take time for you to unlock all of these, days even. We don't have the luxury if we're on the run, and we have to have you gain access to every single document to make a rock-solid case that will lead us to the top of this organization and bring them down."

Ashley pulled away and turned to the table, pulling the laptop close again and typing in the dog's name. Another file opened. "No." Her tone alone ought to brook no argument.

"Why not?"

"Because you said yourself you can't trust someone there. You turn me over and you've got at least one man on the inside who will take me down. I'm safer out here than locked away in there." She pinned his gaze. "You're thinking with your heart, not with your head." She whipped her eyes to the screen before either of them could take the side road to their feelings.

"Okay, true. But it's just a matter of time before we're found again."

"I'm safe for now." She clicked on another photo of a group of young boys kicking a worn soccer ball in a dirty courtyard and bit back a grin. Beckham. Leave it to Sean to find a way to tease her about a celebrity crush at a time like this.

The password revealed another photo, this time of Sean and a group of men, some in civilian clothes and some in uniform, watching the children from the original photo. Ashley was about to slide the image out of the way and move on but stopped, her mind refusing to believe what her eyes saw. Surely she was seeing things, her eyes blurred from exhaustion and too long in front of a screen.

"What?" Ethan caught her hesitation almost before she did. He leaned closer, scanning the picture. "What do you see?"

Ashley pointed at the screen, finger wavering. "Ethan, I know that man."

A broad-shouldered man in khaki pants and a black safari shirt eyed the impromptu soccer match while chatting with another man in an Arab tunic. A very, very familiar smile played on his lips.

She zoomed in. There was no doubt. None. Not in the dark eyes or the even darker hair. Nausea washed over her, dragging with it just how close she'd come to walking into the den of the lion.

"Who is he?" Ethan laid a hand on her back as he leaned forward to see, but the warmth didn't come close to soothing her, not now.

"Sam. Sam Mina. He owns Mina Investments. He's one of my clients."

Disgust ate away at the nausea as Ashley squeezed her eyes shut, images flashing in her memory. "He hired me about six months ago. Right after Sean deployed. I've... I've been to his house for a business dinner. I've been alone with him in his office. He drove me to the airport." She reached for Ethan's hand. "They've been keeping me close all along."

"Probably to use you as a bargaining chip against Sean if they believed he was getting too nosy. If Sam Mina had any idea you were holding the key to what they needed..."

"He called a few days ago and wanted me to come to Albany immediately, but I was in Chicago and told him I'd drive up there when I got home." She buried her head in her shaking hands. "Ethan..."

"They sent the guy to the airport after you because something in Sean's computer tipped them off that he was using you as his backup plan." He rubbed agitated circles on her back. "Sean saved your life by calling me when he did."

But not Katrina's. She nodded, breath bouncing from her hands against her face, trying to erase the vision of those last moments with her cousin. Of Katrina answering the phone and walking toward the bedroom, saying, *"Sam... No, you didn't interrupt anything other than a catch-up session with my cousin."*

"Katrina told him where we were." Ashley's agonized whisper melted against her palm.

"What?"

"She got a phone call this morning from a client. An investment banker named Sam. She tipped him off where we were, totally by accident, and he killed her. He traced from Sean to me, from me to my family..."

Ethan's fingers stuttered to a stop, digging in slightly. "You're sure?"

"I heard it all. And I'm the one who passed her name to him when he asked if I knew anyone he could send some work to. He seemed so...kind." Ashley couldn't stop the visions of her cousin suffering. Of herself walking into Sam Mina's house for dinner and never walking out again. "I talk to him once a week. At least." She lifted her head and sniffed in disgust. "He asked me out once and I turned him down."

Ethan's jaw hardened. "Trying to keep you close." He pulled his hand away and angled himself so he could see her face better. "You okay?"

"No. Sam Mina gained my trust, killed my cousin, took Sean and tried to kill me." She could think about this later, panic about it later. Right now, she wanted to decrypt every single one of Sean's files and prove Sam Mina was behind this.

She wanted to destroy him.

"Tell me what you know about him."

Ashley zoomed out the picture and sat back. "He has

assets overseas, contracts in various countries. All above-board as far as any research I did before I took his company on as a client." She tapped her finger on the mouse pad, and then her head snapped up. She grabbed Ethan's forearm. "I might know where Sean is. Send a message to your guys, even if it might be traced. Tell them to find all of Mina's offices in Afghanistan. He might have Sean at one of them. He's got several, mostly involved in re-building infrastructure." She snapped her fingers. "There was a dam project on one of the rivers. I overheard a guy mention it at his house."

"Got it." Ethan rose and looked down at her. "We're about to locate Sean. I know it." He backed away, glancing at the laptop, then sat again, hard.

"What?" She looked to the computer, eyes still locked on Sam Mina's familiar face.

"Zoom in on that photo again, to the group on the right, the man next to Sean."

Ashley blew up the center of the photo, but Ethan slid the laptop from her hands and manipulated the picture himself, focusing on one man. "Were all of these photos taken in Afghanistan? On this deployment?"

"I don't know for sure but…" She pointed to the lower left of the screen. "The date stamp says this one was taken the deployment before this one, last year. Why?"

"You weren't the only one being watched." He turned the screen to her, jabbing a finger at the bearded, laughing face in the photo, right next to Sean. "We've got bigger problems than we thought."

Her thoughts raced, refused to focus, like a mind slipping into insanity. "Is that…?"

"It's Mitch."

"But…" Ashley's hand went to her mouth and she

leaned forward, refusing to acknowledge what her eyes saw. "But he told me he'd never met Sean."

Ethan drummed his fingers on the table, face hardening into something on the edge of rage. "He lied."

"Maybe he forgot. It was a while ago. Maybe they just crossed paths and—"

"No. No way. It would be too coincidental to have Mina, Sean and Mitchum in the same place at the same time. Nothing in Mitch's records said he was ever in Afghanistan, at least not at the same time as Sean. And definitely not dressed as a civilian."

"Wouldn't Sean have warned you the minute he heard who your new partner was?"

"Not if he knew him by a different name. As far as I know, the man I knew as Craig Mitchum never met Sean. Whoever he's pretending to be here, though? That's a different story."

Ashley refused to believe she'd been alone in her hospital room with a man who'd wanted to do her harm. "The man is dead, Ethan. He died protecting me."

"Did he? Or did he die in a botched attempt to take you? Did he become a liability to whoever he was working with?" Ethan sank into the chair with a groan. "Trust but verify."

"What?"

"Mitch is the one who told me the safe house was compromised and we were forced to change plans, leaving us hanging in the wind with nowhere to run except a contact he set up. Mitch is the one who told me someone was in the building at the hospital, sending us on a blind run straight for the door. If I hadn't changed up the plan when he was shot and still gone to his 'safe' location, we'd have walked right into it. We had the decryption program in hand along with the keys to Sean's box. It was everything they needed, but he couldn't risk taking you from the hospital, where there are security and cameras everywhere, so he fixed it where we'd have to run straight where he wanted us to go.

"Ash—" Ethan pinched the bridge of his nose "—Mitchum is a mole. Which means this is bigger than just one man infiltrating our unit, because our last man on the ground over there went missing before Mitch came on board. This is a coordinated effort." He slammed his palm on the table. "I'm an idiot."

"Ethan, you're not—"

"Yeah, I sort of am. We have to go. All three of us." Ethan shoved the chair out and stood, crossing the kitchen to the foot of the stairs in two long strides. "Tate! We've got to move. You've been compromised."

Ashley stood. Watching. Unbelieving. They couldn't leave. They couldn't run again, not when she'd just started to unravel everything that would free Sean and save her. If he could give her a little more time, everything would be decoded and this would all be over. "Ethan, if we can sit tight an hour or two, I can make some headway on these and—"

A click, a muffled pop, and the house plunged into darkness.

SIXTEEN

Ethan reached for his weapon, grateful the dim light from the laptop screen wasn't enough to allow Ashley to fully see. His mind clicked into operations mode. Protect the asset, secure the evidence, make a clean getaway. "Grab the laptop and the drives. We have to get out of here."

Ashley was in motion before he even finished giving the order.

There was a moment of silence before Tate's feet pounded down the stairs, his silhouette just visible before Ashley shut the laptop and plunged the room into darkness. Tate pressed something cold and jagged into Ethan's hand. "The keys to my Jeep. Get out of here before they find her."

"What about you?"

As Ethan's eyes adjusted, he could make out the bulk of something in Tate's hand.

Tate lofted the object. "Got a motorcycle in the shed for a moment like this." He exhaled loudly and hefted what looked like a go-bag higher on his shoulder. "I'm going to miss this place." But in a moment he was all business, the tremor of his words evidence of an adrenaline high. "I sent a message we've been made and then killed the hard drive by surging the backup battery, so no one should be able to trace what you sent out earlier. Now get Ashley and get moving."

Ethan pulled Ashley closer, not ready to tell her that with Tate's hard drive destroyed, there was no good way to pass on a message about Sean's possible location.

From the front of the house, wood splintered. The door to the kitchen cracked in, as well, glass and wood cacophonous as it skittered across the floor, the silhouette of a man standing in its place.

Ashley screamed.

"Get out!" Tate's voice roared in Ethan's ears just as his bulk jetted across the room and crashed into the shadow in the doorway.

Shouts from the front of the house and pounding feet accentuated the scuffle in front of them.

Ethan reached blindly for Ashley and found her arm, propelling her forward. *Please don't let them have figured out the Jeep is our exit strategy.* It was the only prayer he had time for as they skirted the two men grappling on the floor. He wanted to level a shot at the man wrestling with Tate, but in the dim light he couldn't risk hitting his friend.

One final thud and the larger of the men leaped up and joined them. Tate slapped Ethan on the shoulder and ran full tilt for the shed as Ethan ushered Ashley into the Jeep. She scrambled across the driver's seat, dropped her bag on the floor and buckled tight as Ethan joined her.

The vehicle started without hesitation and Ethan jammed it into Reverse, turning in the seat for a clear view of what lay behind him.

A man appeared in the glow of the taillights, pistol aimed straight at their vehicle.

"Get down!" Ethan grabbed the back of Ashley's head and shoved her forehead to her knees, then gunned the engine into Reverse.

Gunshots shattered the night, overlaying the roar of the Jeep's engine and the rough melody of a motorcycle firing up.

Ethan floored the motor as dull thwacks cracked the vehicle, but the rest of the shots went wild, shattering windows along the side of Tate's house as the gunman leaped out of the way of the Jeep.

In a spray of gravel, Ethan hit the road, rammed the Jeep into gear and spun the tires as he roared down the dark street.

Lights popped on in houses throughout the small, quiet neighborhood.

Just ahead of them, the lights of a motorcycle fishtailed as the bike caught traction, roaring ahead onto the road headed out of town, deeper into Amish country. Tate's contingency plan likely involved a family there where he could lie low.

At least someone in his life had gotten away clean today. Ethan lofted a quick prayer of thanks before checking the mirrors and deciding on his own escape route. He wished he had a backup plan, but Tate's place had already been one of his last resorts. If Tate's house was compromised, so was every other option. The best thing to do was to hit the highway and go as hard as they could. He hadn't seen what their attackers were driving, but it wasn't difficult to guess the engine was more powerful than his.

Behind him, a vehicle spun out of Tate's driveway and shot forward in pursuit. In about a minute those men would be on their tail.

Ethan drummed the steering wheel and, as he came to an intersection, killed the headlights.

Beside him, Ashley lifted her head. "You're driving blind?" Her voice was weak, but it didn't indicate the panic he'd come to listen for, even though shots had been fired.

"Keeps them from tracking my taillights." The move

was risky, but when he turned off the main road, he didn't want anyone to follow. With the moon obscured by clouds, it wouldn't grant them invisibility, but it would make the dark gray Jeep a whole lot harder to spot.

Sure enough, the headlights behind him hesitated at an intersection before accelerating toward them again.

Ethan passed two more side roads before he took a blind left without slowing, throwing Ashley against the door. She muffled a scream and braced against the dash.

The Jeep slowed as Ethan tried to keep an eye on the dark road that glowed faintly in the starlight. He sensed more than saw the opening in the woods and took it, bouncing a few feet along a dirt road. They were boxed in, but there was no other place to hide. He unbuckled his seat belt and laid a hand on his weapon. "Get ready to run if they come this way." They'd have to hide in the woods—again—but they were out of options.

Ashley's seat belt clicked and she leaned forward, hefting the laptop bag onto her lap. "Okay."

Through the trees, Ethan watched. It was only a few seconds before headlights slowed at the intersection, then roared forward without turning.

Ethan released his pistol and allowed his muscles to relax. He'd wait sixty seconds, reverse, then double back toward Sackets Harbor. They'd stick to the less-traveled roads parallel to the river until they found a quiet place for a couple of hours. Ashley needed time to finish decoding enough of Sean's intel to obtain a search warrant and move the investigation forward.

Trouble was, he had no idea where he was going.

Ashley pushed hard against the seat, waiting for the familiar panic to burn in her spine and push out through every pore in her body.

She prepared to fight hard against it, but…nothing. Her eyes drifted shut. She felt nothing. No fear, no sadness, no joy, no pain, no nothing. She'd sunk into a place worse than the panic, a place where nothing could touch her.

Not even Ethan Kincaid.

Life was a movie. Everything around her detached and she was a passive observer, unaffected by anything outside of herself. It was like listening under water, everything muffled and hard to hear, hard to process. The sensation could be exhaustion…but what if this time she'd been pushed too far and she never resurfaced? What if she stayed dead inside forever?

Ethan had been driving in silence for about fifteen minutes, taking turn after turn on roads that seemed to lead to nowhere. He reached over as she moved, laying a hand on the back of her neck. "You okay?"

"Fine." She leaned into his touch for a second before she pulled away and his hand dropped to the stick shift. "Where are we going?"

"I have no idea." Ethan shook his head. "I'm out of safe houses unless we head for the city, and if Tate's house has been compromised, none of them are secure."

"Where will Tate go?" Her cousin was already gone. She couldn't bear to think of someone else dead because they'd tried to help her.

"I don't know." Ethan shifted his hands on the steering wheel and propped his elbow on the door, dragging a hand through his hair. "We've all got our own places to run, places we don't tell because of situations like this."

"And yours is…?"

"Too far from here to do us any good. This isn't my usual area of operations. I mean, I know the lay of the land from the time we were stationed here, but it's been a while. I'm here now because…" He cleared his throat and fell silent, the headlights of a passing car playing across his face.

Because of you. The unspoken words breached the wall holding her emotions, opening a crack that loosed her tongue, caused her brain to forget it needed to filter everything she said to Ethan Kincaid. "You could have sent someone else, could have let another team handle this."

"Sean and I are the ones who dragged you into this. This is my mission and that makes it my job to ensure your safety. And I didn't want to trust anyone else with you. You're too important. Ash, I'm sorry. You could be home right now asleep in your own bed if I hadn't let Sean talk me into passing all of this on to you without your knowledge."

The trees outside whipped by in the dark, ghosts of their daylight selves. Ashley allowed herself a moment to dream. To be home right now would be wonderful.

Except something would be missing.

Could she honestly, really say she'd reject the safety of her life forty-eight hours ago for this? For being beside Ethan again?

"Hey." His hand crept across the space between them, hesitated, then found hers. "You tensed up. Need me to stop so you can have a minute? I think we're far enough away from those guys to find a place to pull off."

Tears pressed against the backs of her eyes as she squeezed his hand tighter. "No."

"Then what do you need from me?"

It was a loaded question, even if he didn't realize it. For the first time in memory she didn't feel fear, even though there was every reason in the world to do so. When he touched her, she didn't feel so dead that the world passed her by. The warmth started in her hand, crept up her arm and stole into her soul. No matter she didn't want him to be, no matter she'd fought hard against it because God would eventually take him, Ethan Kincaid was everything she wanted, her safe place, the anchor she needed in a world out of control. That was why the gunshots at the house hadn't registered.

She might have him for only a short time, but for now, he was with her.

"You've already given me everything." Ashley sniffled in dry amusement. "Chances are, you and Sean saved me by sending those files. It put your eyes on me a lot sooner than if you hadn't, got you to my side a whole lot quicker to counter their move against me." She squeezed his hand, wishing she'd never have to let go. "Seems like you're always there right when I need you most. You've saved my life. More than once. You're..." How could she tell him? "You're what keeps me safe."

Ethan froze. It was as though her words hit the pause button on his entire existence.

"Don't, Ashley. It's a lie." His voice was choked. He cleared his throat and tried again. "Don't put me in this position. I can't save you."

There was an instant where she had to process the words before she pulled her hand from his, her leg muscles stiffening. She brushed hair from her face. "But you have saved me. Every time. That's no lie."

"I also almost got you killed. Every time you've needed to be rescued, it's been my fault. I should have said this at the house." He huffed a disgusted sigh, one that knocked the wind from her sails. "You're looking for a rock, and I'm not it. I'm going to fail you."

"But—"

"No. Listen. I want to be everything to you, more than

you know. But what I want is for you to want me, not for you to need me. If you need me, if you latch on to me because I'm the stability in your life, then, one day, I'm going to disappoint you, and when I do, it will devastate you."

"What?"

"Ash, I refuse to be an idol." The words leaked regret that tore at her.

"You're not."

"You're setting me up in a position no man can fill. I can't keep you safe or be the guiding force in your life. Only God can do that."

"God hasn't done a very good job with my life."

"You don't really believe that. Think about it. He's allowed everything you've tried to lean on, every place you've run to for shelter, to be stripped away. Why do you think that is?"

Ashley pulled her arms tight over her chest. This humiliation, this rejection, could stop anytime.

"Because He's trying to teach you to lean on Him. No matter what the illusion of safety anywhere else is, He's really the only thing that can have first place in your life. Ash, He's calling you back."

"Stop." There was no way God cared whether or not she came to Him. His sole interest lay in wrecking her life.

But Ethan wasn't finished. "Okay, answer me this, and you answer it with everything in you because right now is not the time to lie to me."

Something in his tone stopped her from arguing, even though every ounce of her being groaned under his recrimination and rejection. It crushed her. She'd laid herself out there and he was telling her she wasn't good enough, she needed to be fixed.

"When we were pinned down at the post office, you

were a rock, something I never expected from you with shots fired, not with all Sean's told me and all I've seen. Why? Because I was there?"

Ashley opened her mouth to speak but Ethan held his hand up to silence her.

"If it was me you were leaning on, you never would have crossed the parking lot ahead of me and gone into those woods alone. You'd have clung to me like a toddler looking for her daddy. Where was your strength coming from?" He pulled his attention from the road to pin her gaze, eyes glittering in the dim light from the instrument panel. "Where were you leaning?"

Ashley's hands fluttered in front of her. "On the moment. On the next thing. On anything but…" Her mind raced through the memory and landed on one thing. *Lord, keep us safe.*

She'd prayed. And that wasn't the only time. When pinned down with nowhere to turn, it wasn't Ethan she'd looked to.

"Ash, I don't have to be in your head to know what you did. You didn't have to say it out loud. What I do know is, before you were shot, Jesus was your everything, and that doesn't die. You can shove Him away, but He won't go away. In the clinch, you knew where to go, and He answered you. And until you get it straight I'm not the one—"

A shrill trill cut off his words and made Ashley jump. "What was that?"

"My phone. Tate's the only one with the number. And he wouldn't risk the call unless something was bad wrong."

SEVENTEEN

Ethan pulled onto the shoulder of the road. If Tate was calling, something had gone way off the rails. He forced himself into rational thought as he yanked the phone from his pocket and read the unfamiliar number. *Lord, let this be a wrong number. Anything.* Anything but his buddy in danger. Anything but one more life in the balance because of this mission. He swallowed hard and punched the button, settling the phone at his ear. "Yeah?"

"Captain Kincaid. So nice to hear your voice."

In all of his life, Ethan had never actually felt his blood run cold. He recognized the voice. It was the same smooth, calculated voice he'd heard over his phone just before gunshots had taken Mitchum's life.

"How did you get this number?" If they'd found Tate and hurt him, he'd turn this Jeep around and deal with all of this himself.

"You are a hard man to find, but not as impossible as you might think. The fact is, we are in contact. And the other fact is…you know we have Staff Sergeant Turner. You are looking in the wrong place. You know your time is growing short. We will find you and Miss Colson."

Ethan said nothing, taking control of the conversation by letting the deep voice on the other end think it held all of the power. He glanced at the clock, calculating how long it would take to triangulate the signal to his cell phone. Even with the latest technology, they had a little bit of time.

"I will simply say this. If you do not stop running and turn over every piece of data you have on our operation… If you pass along anything that would prevent us from reaching our goals… Things will get very, very uncomfortable for Staff Sergeant Turner. And, Captain? I can assure you. We will never, ever stop hunting for you or for the girl. You know quite well if we can find you, then we can find her. You also know what will happen to her when we do."

Ethan knew quite well what these men were capable of. He fought to keep the knowledge from his voice. "Well, I'd suggest you bring an army with you when you show up."

A chuckle menaced across the line. "It is all very simple. You bring me the information I want so it can stop being a concern to our business interests, and I will return your associate to you and call my men off Ashley Colson. You have my word. She may be the key to all of your intelligence, but she is no threat to us if the data you hold is off of the table."

Ethan's nostrils flared as he fought to control his voice lest the man on the other end of the line hear his anger. "I want proof of life for Sean Turner."

"That is understandable and quite a simple matter."

A pause, distant mumbling, a small scrape and then another voice.

"Ethan. It's Sean."

Ethan's pulse picked up at the familiar sound of Sean's voice. He turned to Ashley, lips pressed in a grim line.

After what happened to Mitchum, there was no way he was going to put this on speaker. "Talk to me."

"I'm fine. Good. Nearly got away once."

"I knew you'd try."

"Keep her safe, Ethan. I think we both know how you feel about—"

"Enough." The first man cut in. "Are you satisfied?"

Ethan kept his mouth shut. If he didn't talk, it would force the other guy to speak just to fill the dead air. With any answered prayer, he'd slip up and tell them too much.

Seconds ticked by. Ethan was running out of time before the man broke the silence. "You know we do not play games, do you not? We want those files or we want Colson. Sooner rather than later. Do you need further convincing?" The sound of a gunshot shattered through the line, jerking Ethan's head as Sean screamed in pain. "That was his shoulder. Refuse to cooperate and it will be much more." There was a metallic buzz as the line broke and the call ended.

Ethan's knees turned to water. Sean was alive but suffering at the hands of brutal men who held no concern for human life. The echo of the shot ricocheted in his head. He slammed the flip phone shut and clenched it tightly.

Ashley laid a hand on his arm. "What?" Concern edged with fear in her voice. "Is Tate okay? Is Sean?"

"Tate's fine." His voice drew taut, nerves choking him. For the moment there was no way he could tell her Sean had been shot. It might be one shock too many. His finger tapped the phone. He glanced at the clock. Nearly six. The sun was already coloring the horizon. "They must have found a way to trace the calls coming in to Tate's cell phone, which isn't out of the realm of possibility since Mitch knew him. There's no other way they could have gotten my number."

"What did they say?"

Ethan shook his head, not wanting to pass on desperate information. But she'd demand an answer if he didn't give her one. "They still have Sean, but they've tipped their hand. I know where he is."

Ashley sucked in a breath. "Where?"

"The man on the phone was the same guy who shot Mitch. He said we were looking in the wrong place. He let me speak to Sean… He's been brought to the States. Does Mina Investments have any holdings stateside that you know of?"

"I'm sure they do, but I dealt with computer networking and security, not directly with any of their files. His house is practically a compound, though."

"That would be a huge risk. If anyone located Sean on Mina's personal property, he'd have no way to explain it. What about his offices?"

"Near the edge of town. Shares a building with a few government satellite offices."

"Makes it easier to make friends and contacts. He wants to keep those contracts coming in, but it makes taking Sean there a risk."

Ashley laid her head against the headrest and closed her eyes. "When I was there last time, I was in his office doing a security update. One of the big guys came in and said something about the new warehouse close by making it a lot easier to move construction equipment because it was right on the railroad tracks."

"If I was Sam Mina, and I was going to hold someone against their will, that would be the likely place. It's easy to say someone broke into your warehouse and used it to hold a hostage without your knowledge."

Ethan tapped the steering wheel with his thumb. They were a couple of hours from Albany, but his gut said Sean was there. It was possible the bad guys wanted him to bring Ashley to Sean, then use her to show Sean they meant business, to get him to tell them everything he knew. Ethan shuddered to think what they would do to Ashley in such a situation.

Well, if they'd burned his phone, he might as well use it and take the risk someone would hear his plan. Ethan dialed the number he knew too well and prayed for loyalty on the other end.

"This is Franklin."

If Colonel Ron Franklin was the mole, they were in trouble too deep to get out of anyway. Ethan had to trust him. "Colonel, it's Kincaid."

Franklin paused. "You'd better have a good reason for making contact."

"I need a team in Albany. At a warehouse owned by Sam Mina, Mina Investments or any company related to him. We have everything we need." Short. To the point. Not too much information but enough to rat out a mole if one was listening.

"You're sure you have everything?"

"Everything. And they have everyone." *Let him understand...*

"You sure?"

"As sure as I can be. And I need gear."

There was a short rustle of movement. "ETA for advance team is 0900. I'll make sure you're equipped and put a hostage-rescue team in place. Reconnect in two hours."

Ethan glanced at the clock. Three hours until the team arrived. He'd pull surveillance until they got there. This early in the day, they'd likely have to wait for Mina to arrive anyway.

"Out." Ethan slapped the phone shut, popped the back and pulled the battery out.

"Not going to destroy the phone?"

"Pretty impossible to track with the battery out."

Ashley looked away and scanned the windshield as Ethan edged the Jeep onto the road again. "So I guess we're going to Albany."

"And if anyone was listening, they heard and will come looking for you there. You're staying in a hotel. Once the advance team hits the ground, I'll send someone after you." It wasn't his first or most comfortable choice, but there was no way he was taking her into the danger zone.

"Absolutely not."

He'd expected the blowback. "There's no other option. And as long as no one's following us, placing you in a random location is our best bet to keep you safe."

"Shoving me out of the way alone isn't doing anything but putting me in danger. How do you know I'll be safe without you?"

"I'll give you my gun."

"You know I won't take it."

It had been stupid of him to offer his weapon, but the idea of leaving her alone and defenseless was too much for his common sense. "Then you come up with a better suggestion. I have to meet the team in Albany to hand over the files you've decrypted, because we can't risk sending them electronically and we can't go in without just cause. Higher-ups are going to want to see proof before they'll let a team go in and take Sam Mina."

"You know those files are useless without me. You can hand me and the drives over at the same time. In Albany."

Ethan jabbed a finger at the bag nestled at her feet. "Then open your laptop. You've got a couple of hours to decode as much as you can so we can build a case for this raid, but I'm not taking you there with me. Mina knows who you are."

"I'll stay out of sight."

"It's dangerous."

Ashley rolled her eyes to the canvas ceiling of the Jeep, which flapped even louder in the silence between them. "Ethan, this is Sean we're talking about. He's practically my brother. I'll never be able to decode several hundred files that quickly. Your only hope of saving anybody is if I go with you and continue to work right up until the handover. You don't even know if Mina's in town. You could call a team in and find out he's in Baltimore or San Diego. Think, Ethan. There's no one else who can get him where you need him to be."

"What do you mean?"

"He's called me under the guise of having me come and do more work for his company. All I have to do is contact him and tell him I'm in town, ready to meet."

"Ashley, no. No way. If we do have someone listening, they just heard me call in a team. If not, his guys have tried more than once to take you. They know you're with me and there's no telling what they learned from Mitch. They know you've been to the post office and they know you have those drives. Even if they didn't, it would be suspicious if you were 'business as usual' with all that's happening right now. You forget, this guy is hunting you, even if he doesn't know you've figured him out."

"Then I tell him I know he's behind this. All I have to do is say I want to deal, that I've slipped you and want to trade the information for Sean's life."

"I say no."

"And I say there's no other way to guarantee he'll be exactly where you want him to be when you bring a team in. Otherwise, you have to pull surveillance for who knows how long until he shows up, because I'll guarantee you he's lying low right now."

Ethan pounded the steering wheel with the side of his hand, the shock of impact jolting up his arm and clearing his head. As much as he wanted to stash her out of harm's way, she was right. The only way to save her was to expose her.

Sean and he had effectively backed her into a corner with no way out except through the fire.

"We're here." Ethan's voice cut through the concentration she'd been laser-focusing on the computer screen in front of her since he'd pointed the Jeep toward Albany. She'd cracked dozens of new files, but hundreds more still waited.

Looking up, Ashley scanned the area, a pang of familiarity mingling with the dizziness from not focusing on the road while riding in the car. It took a second to clear her thoughts.

The low, glass, two-story building housing Mina Investments looked like any other structure on the block. She scanned the area, the large parking lot just beginning to fill as the workday began.

"Tell me everything you know." Ethan's hand draped over the steering wheel, his focus on the building, taking in everything that could help his team when they showed up.

Ashley closed her eyes, trying to remember the layout of the offices. "There's a lobby when you go in. Lots of glass, plants, seating areas scattered around. A sandwich shop and coffee bar to the right just past the entrance."

"Security?"

"None other than a few private security guards milling around. No one checks people coming in and out, no main receptionist or security checkpoint."

"Hmm. He's pretty confident nobody will figure him out if he's in a place like that."

"Probably didn't want to raise any red flags. There're a lot of offices in the building, most of them government contractors and the like, so you'll have to be careful how you go in, watch for civilians. His block of offices is through the lobby then to the left. There's a receptionist just as you step into his section. But…" Why had this not set off alarms before now? "Lots of very big guys work for him. The kind you see on TV. They aren't really doing anything, just hanging around."

"Personal security." Ethan pressed his lips together and handed Ashley the phone he'd picked up at a truck stop outside of town, ensuring the number was different from the one Mina's man already knew. "Are you sure you want to make this call?"

She nodded. "I want this over. I want Sean safe. And I want to go home."

Ethan's brown gaze flickered, then hardened. "Make the call. Before I change my mind."

Ashley dialed the number she'd memorized while in talks with her biggest client and waited, trying not to think of where he'd earned the money he'd paid her.

The phone rang three times and went to voice mail, Mina's slight accent sending a cold shiver down her spine even as a recording. His accent had once sounded like her company's future. Now it slithered death into her soul. She steeled herself for the beep. "Mr. Mina, this is Ashley Colson. I have some things you might be interested in and I'm willing to discuss them with you if we can reach an agreement." She clicked the end button and held the phone out to Ethan, who watched her grimly.

"When he calls, let him drive the bus. Don't tell him where you want to meet. In fact, say as little as possible. Remember, you're scared of the big, bad man who has your friend. Don't pretend you have any control at all."

No control at all. The last place she ever wanted to be.

The phone in her hand vibrated before the fear could jolt her.

Ethan nodded, his hands fisted against his thighs.

Ashley clicked to answer and pressed the phone to her ear. "Hello?"

"Who is with you, Ms. Colson?" The slick sound of Sam Mina's voice was low and menacing, something she'd never heard before.

"No one."

He chuckled. "Now, you and I both know this is not true. My men have tried to contact you multiple times for a private conversation, but you never seem to be alone."

His men had tried to contact her? How polite and innocent. Ashley bit her tongue. This guy was good. "I'm alone now. And I'm in Albany."

"Out from under the umbrella of your protection? I doubt that very much."

"Some people don't understand the value of negotiation. They're willing to let the system work, no matter how much time it takes. But, Mr. Mina, I just…" Her voice cracked from the strain, but she went with it, playing to her weakness. "I just want my friend, so I'm on my own, with the information you need. And I'll give it to you if—"

"And what makes you think I know where this friend of yours is? We are merely business acquaintances. It is you I work with, not him. I do not even know this person."

Ashley wanted to scream at the pace of the conversation, at the nonchalance in the man's voice. She wanted to reach through the phone and strangle him, to do anything to rattle his cage. "You know many of my friends. After all, you hired my cousin to do your company's taxes. And I'm sure you've met my friend before. I have a photo of you with him and Craig Mitchum at a youth soccer game, I believe."

Ethan winced and reached for the phone, but Ashley ignored him. If she'd gone too far, she'd gone too far. At this point she'd do anything to end this with Mina shackled as he deserved, even if it meant tipping her hand.

The line fell silent. She'd rattled him and now he knew she'd decoded the photos.

"My office. Ninety minutes. And bring your files with you." The line died.

Ashley slumped in the seat, letting the phone drop into her lap. She'd set this thing in motion and now there was no way out without sacrificing all three of them.

EIGHTEEN

The digits on Ethan's watch finally rolled to 0900, bringing an end to the silent waiting. The hours had slogged by in a mixture of exhaustion and apprehension. He inserted the battery into his burner phone and waited for the device to power up.

While Ashley had spent the time deciphering passwords, Ethan watched in silence, leery of saying anything to her when his anger and frustration bubbled so close to the surface his skin burned. She never should have told Mina they'd already unlocked some of the documents. Now he knew she'd seen the evidence.

Ashley's life was worthless in that man's eyes.

Ethan bit down on his lip. No, forget being nice. Ashley needed to hear what he had to say, to know she'd gone too far. "If you step one foot in there, you'll never come out alive."

Her fingers paused on the keys. Then her head came up slowly, almost as though she'd forgotten he was in the vehicle. "Out of where?"

"Mina's office. He'll kill you, then Sean, not only because you can unlock the evidence but because you've seen it. It's in your head, and he'll want every loose end tied up. You never should have told him—"

"He wasn't afraid of me until I said that."

The matter-of-fact way she said it roared the simmering fire of his anger into a boil.

"You just had to have control, didn't you?"

The bang of the laptop slapping shut ricocheted through the vehicle as Ashley whirled in the seat, fire in her gaze. "No. I had to knock him off balance, make him stop thinking with his head and start thinking with his fear. I'm not stupid, Ethan. I trained to play this game, too, remember? And I'm pretty familiar with the way fear can completely short-circuit rational thought." She clutched the laptop tight. "I have no intention of walking into his office, and if you thought I did, then it's pretty telling about what you think of me and my level of intelligence."

The accusation cut too close to the truth, cooling his ire into resignation. Ashley was in more danger now than she had been all along, and the situation was spinning to the point Ethan could no longer control the outcome. "He'll never stop looking for you now."

"Which is why you have to take him down. Today."

It was foolishness to think this would all end with one man's arrest, but before he could make another argument, his cell chimed with a text. Team in place. The address was less than two miles away. Ethan started the Jeep and pulled out, ready to meet his assigned team but reluctant to hand Ashley over to anyone else's care. If there was a way to be two places at once, he'd take it about now.

"Where are we going?"

"The advance team is in place along with an FBI hostage-rescue team, waiting for us to hand over the files you've decoded, which should be enough to get us clearance to go in."

"Then what?"

"You're staying with one of them."

"What about you?" The fact she didn't argue spoke to the fear dampening her emotions.

Ethan's grip on the steering wheel tightened. She would definitely have an issue with the next part. "I'm going in with them." Whether the team wanted him to or not, he was going to be on hand to make certain Sam Mina faced justice for the lives he'd destroyed.

"Ethan, no." Ashley reached for his arm, grabbing his biceps. Her fingers dug deep into muscle. "Stay out of there. He'll target you first."

He shook her off. If she begged too hard, he'd listen, cave in to her the way he always did. "You'll be safe. I know at least one guy on the team I can trust. He'll keep an eye on you. We'll keep you out of the way, far from us. All of Mina's men will be focused elsewhere, especially if he's gotten wind we're coming. He'll pool all his resources together, right where we want them." When she started to speak again, he held up a hand. "You can't talk me out of this. Don't even try." *Because if you try, you'll succeed.*

"Okay, then."

That was almost too easy. "You're not planning on gearing up and coming in behind me, are you?"

"No." She reopened the laptop and went to work, fingers flying faster than before. "I'll transfer everything I've decrypted to one of the drives so I can continue working while you're…busy."

"I'm sure we have enough for now." She was bound to be exhausted with nearly a day's worth of sleepless hours behind her. "Why don't you take it easy for a little while? We'll have this wrapped up by lunchtime." He hoped.

"No. I can't sit and do nothing. And there's no way I can relax while you're in there. I'll keep working. And praying. Hard."

Praying? Ethan wanted to ask what she meant but before he could, a black sedan and three Suburban SUVs came into view. Three plainclothes agents merged with the hostage-rescue team turned out in tactical gear. The group huddled at the back of one of the Suburbans. In the small warehouse parking lot, they looked harmless, but Ethan knew they likely packed more firepower than most people would see in their whole lives.

Ethan pulled to a stop close to a long metal building and waited for them to recognize him before he shut off the vehicle. "Stay here." He forced himself not to touch her. If he did, he'd never get out of the vehicle. The best thing he could do right now was to get his head in the game and his mind off Ashley Colson. Doing anything else could jeopardize the operation. With effort, he built the wall around his emotions. "We'll take down Mina, then find Sean."

She pressed the thumb drive into his palm, her fingers warm and electric around his, almost making him rethink his plan to go in with the team. "I hope you're right."

So did he. If he was wrong, they could all be dead within the hour.

"Stay in the vehicle. No matter what." Without looking back, Ethan opened the door and stepped out of the Jeep to meet with the men at the Suburban. He shook the hand of the man who appeared to be in charge and handed him the drive, then jerked a thumb toward Ashley.

One of the men, tall and broad-shouldered with dark hair, broke away from the group. He headed for the Jeep, motioning for Ashley to roll the window down. He stuck his hand through the space. "Jack Winters. I've known Ethan since Officer Candidate School."

From across the parking lot, Ethan caught her eye,

nodded, then looked away. She swallowed her disappointment at his sudden coldness and extended her hand to Jack Winters. "Ashley Colson. You're my bodyguard?"

He smiled an easy smile. "So to speak. Although I think Kincaid's more worried about you following on the mission than someone coming after you."

It wouldn't be the first time she'd bucked his orders and, despite his pulling away from her, she smiled. "Wise man."

Winters jerked his chin toward the group. "I'm going to finish the briefing. Then I'll be back."

Before he could walk away Ashley grabbed for him, catching the edge of his shirt in her fingers. "What about…?" How much was she allowed to say, even allowed to know, about Sean?

Winters gave a cautious smile. "We have reason to believe he's close. And alive. Other than that, I can't tell you." He patted her hand, extricated his arm from her grasp and walked toward the group, saying something to Ethan as he passed.

Ethan didn't react. Instead he took the vest someone handed him and strapped it on, then reached into the SUV for more of what looked like body armor. He was fully outfitted in tactical gear, helmet in hand, before he turned and his eyes met hers.

They held for a long time, Ethan's eyes searching hers across the space between them, looking for something.

Instead of joining the group, he crossed the small space between them and came to her, resting his crossed forearms on the open window, his shoulders even broader in the gear he wore. "Plan change. They're sending a smaller team in after Mina. Aerial surveillance thinks they've found Sean. We're going to bring him out."

"Really?" To have it all over, not just Mina's capture

but Sean's rescue in one morning, would be more than an answered prayer.

Ethan nodded, eyes serious. "There's another team working on a more secure location for you, so you might be moved before I get back, but I'll come to you. Will you be all right until then?"

Ashley could hardly speak. She waved a trembling hand toward Winters. "I've got a security detail on me. I'll be fine." *It's you I'm worried about.* If Mina had been tipped off by someone listening in on the unit's secure line, he knew they were coming. And he was not the type of man to step back and let a team of highly trained FBI agents waltz into his territory without a fight.

"It's all going to work out. And when it does…" Ethan reached in and squeezed her hand. "You and I need to talk."

One of the agents stepped up to Ethan. "We're a go on entering the building."

Giving her fingers one last squeeze, Ethan pressed a kiss to her forehead, then walked away without looking back, climbing into the passenger seat of a Suburban, game face firmly in place. He was focused on the mission ahead. Nothing else.

But Ashley couldn't stop thinking about his last words. *Lord, bring him back safely.* She rolled her eyes skyward. *Please.*

This time, she hoped God was listening because she had no control over this situation. None. There was no other hope but to surrender.

He's trying to teach you to lean on Him. No matter what the illusion of safety anywhere else is, He's really the only thing that can have first place in your life. Ethan's words, Tate's story… They teased her thoughts as two of the SUVs pulled out and Winters walked over to stand beside the passenger side of the Jeep, keeping watch on the area.

God hadn't let her die in behind a duplex. He hadn't let those men kill Sean on sight but had kept him alive this far. He'd protected Ethan and her every step of this journey, even in the moments when it seemed as though they were backed to the cliff's edge with no way out. Every step, He'd watched over her.

So if she was still alive after everything, what was she living for? To be terrified of life outside her front door? To hide behind a computer screen and miss out on the best gifts she'd been given?

Or to harness her talents, hone her skills and follow an entirely different dream?

Maybe even a dream that included Ethan Kincaid, a man who would leave for parts unknown for weeks at a time, but whose heart would stay true no matter what. She could let go and love Ethan, taking the risk she might lose him but trusting God each morning to get them through another day. Or she could walk away from him now and have her heart go with him, piece by shattered piece.

Ashley laid her head back and closed her eyes. Could she do that? She'd have to trust God would keep Ethan safe, and if He didn't, she'd be okay. It was better than losing him the moment this mission ended.

Her head dipped forward. Even now, his life, her life, Sean's life…they were all in His hands. Sitting in a borrowed Jeep, completely without control, Ashley surrendered.

"You up for this, Captain? My understanding is you've been on the run for days." One of the younger agents— James, someone had called him—leaned up between the front seats, a wry grin taking the sting from his words.

Ethan tapped a finger against the young agent's eye protection, then tightened the chin strap of his own helmet. With the amount of adrenaline thundering through his veins, he could keep going for another week. If a team was about to rescue Sean, he was going to be part of it. "I'm fine. You worry about yourself."

James threw a mock salute and settled back in his seat.

"Don't mind him." Agent Klass allowed himself a quick smile. "He's just excited we allowed him to tag along."

"Whatever." James lobbed the word to them. "You act like I'm a kid."

"You aren't? You shaved this week?" Klass laughed. "The young ones just love a good adrenaline rush."

Ethan stretched out his neck, muscles tense from the short ride to the warehouse. A trace from headquarters located a second company with ties to Mina Investments that had recently purchased the property. A quick sweep earlier this morning by a helicopter with infrared cameras showed three heat signatures deep inside the city-block-size building, two walking, one sitting in the center.

"Who's going to take down Mina?" Ethan had been disappointed not to be going to the offices to face off with Mina himself, but he understood the issue. There were too many civilians in the building to send in a full crew and risk a shoot-out. Instead, hostage rescue would hit the warehouse while two agents simultaneously stepped in and took Sam Mina into custody. The information Ashley had decoded provided more than enough evidence to justify both arms of the operation.

"Weber and Stephens. Don't worry about either of them tipping him off." Klass lowered his voice. "I was briefed on the mole. Weber and Stephens were vetted again, and this team has no connection to anyone at your unit." Klass raised his voice so the rest of the vehicle's occupants could hear him. "A quick sweep didn't reveal any security cameras on the outside of the building, but that doesn't mean they aren't there. Our snipers are in place with a team set up on the perimeter. Stay low, get our man and get out. Keep his two guards alive if at all possible. And remember, Turner's injured. We're looking at a carry-out."

Ethan tightened his grip on his rifle and checked to make sure his sidearm was in easy reach at his thigh. Getting Sean out would be tough if he was in as bad a shape as Ethan feared, requiring the loss of at least one gunner to buddy-carry him out. He bit back a grin. Knowing Sean, he'd make it out under his own power even if he had to crawl over every inch of the warehouse floor.

The Suburban eased to a stop outside a loading entrance, where a small door stood beside massive exterior garage doors. On the earlier sweep of the area, one of their men had disabled the lock, leaving the entrance ready for them to breach.

Klass reached for his door handle as the five men in the back took their positions, ready to exit at his command. Two more men stayed behind with the communications equipment.

Adjusting the mike at his mouth, Klass nodded. "Go."

The team filed out and headed for the door on silent feet, Ethan bringing up the rear, stepping backward up the stairs alongside another member of the team, watching for any surprises. They gained quick entry through the door and separated into two groups of four, each taking one side of the warehouse. Ethan's team crept along the wall, their boots nearly silent on the concrete as they crept toward a makeshift wall of boxes near the center of the building.

Fingers of adrenaline crawled across Ethan's skin at the silence of the cavernous space. There was nowhere to take cover, nowhere to hide if anyone stepped out from behind those boxes or out of a hidden doorway and started shooting. Something felt wrong, as though the building held its breath and waited. It crept up his spine and tickled the hairs at the back of his neck.

Ethan's trigger finger tensed as he focused his attention in the direction from which they'd come. Shooting was the last thing they wanted, especially with no way to see on the other side of those boxes. One stray bullet would be all it took to injure or kill Sean.

As they neared the box wall, the team stopped, mirroring the movements of their counterparts on the other side of the room.

With two fingers, Klass motioned the men into position, forming a half circle around the target area. He held a fist in the air and everyone stood motionless, silent, waiting for the call. With a rotation of his arm, Klass moved them forward like a machine.

He breached the wall first. "Hands in the air!"

The warehouse became a flurry of motion and dust as the team converged on the area, rifles lifted.

No frightened shouts echoed. No gunfire sounded. The building stood eerily quiet as the echoes of Klass's command died off of the metal walls.

Ethan lowered his weapon and stepped around the corner to find the rest of the men staring at exactly what he saw.

Three chairs, a table, a severed rope…

Nothing save a puddle of blood under the nearest chair.

NINETEEN

Ashley looked up from the computer screen as the battery gave out, cutting to black as she'd been about to type the name of their high school mascot into the program. She'd lost count of how many passwords she'd cracked since Ethan and the team pulled out, though her progress had definitely grown slower. Fatigue and worry wreaked havoc on her memories, making it harder to decipher Sean's codes.

Across the small parking lot, part of the team still worked at the back of the remaining vehicle, intent on things Ashley couldn't see. Ethan and the men with him had been gone more than half an hour and, to her knowledge, not a word had come to Winters on the radio. It was taking too long.

His reflection in the sideview mirror hadn't changed since the last time she'd looked. He still stood there, pulling surveillance, head always in motion as he watched. With nothing else to occupy her, Ashley prayed for the hundredth time since the men left on their mission.

"Come again?" From outside the vehicle, Winters's voice drifted in.

Ashley straightened and pivoted in the seat to watch him speak.

"Okay. All clear here. Keep me posted. Out." He turned and found her watching him, his mouth a grim line.

Ashley leaned across the passenger seat and rolled down the window as he approached. "What? Is Ethan okay? Sean? What?"

"We've got a secure location. You'll be moved soon."

Ashley wasn't buying it. "That's not the only thing you just heard. Is Ethan…? Is the team okay?"

"The team is fine." Winters hooked the radio into place on his belt and looked toward the men on the other side of the lot, clearly wishing he was with them. "The building was empty. They swept the entire place and found evidence of occupation, but no one's there now. Whoever it was spooked and ran."

Ashley's heart dropped into her stomach and hardened into stone, leaving an ache that nearly doubled her over. "Somebody tipped them off we knew their exact location. All I told them was we were coming to Albany."

"Looks that way. They're sweeping the outside of the building to see if they can find anything. Then they'll come here." Winters met her eye for a moment and then returned to his surveillance. "I'm sorry." He was back at his post before she could respond.

Ashley slipped into the driver's seat and dropped her head to the steering wheel, fighting tears. She'd been so sure Ethan would save the day, so sure God would answer and bring her best friend and the man she loved to her before the sun reached its peak in the sky. Now they were back where they'd started, no closer to the end of this than they had been when Ethan rescued her at the airport.

It's not over. The words, which should have been menacing, drifted from her mind to her soul, soothing her, bringing peace. It wasn't over. She was still alive and so was Ethan, and as long as there was breath in them, there was a chance to rescue Sean. They might not know where he was, but God did. And His eyes never closed.

Voices drifted forward from the back of the Jeep and Ashley lifted her head. The team couldn't have returned already, could they?

"We're ready to move Ms. Colson." It wasn't Winters, but something about the voice was familiar.

Ashley looked into the side mirror as Winters reached out and took some papers from someone, a man too tall for his face to reflect in the mirror. "Glad we've got a more secure location. It's hard to keep a 360 eye here. Good they sent you, though you should have been on the team calling the shots with Kincaid, shouldn't you?"

"We needed someone we could trust to move Ms. Colson. You can join your team now. I'll take it from here."

Winters jogged toward the van as the newcomer stepped up to the passenger door, finally allowing Ashley a clear view of his face.

"Good to see you again." Craig Mitchum leveled a gun through the window, straight at Ashley's chest. "I think it goes without saying that if you call for help, I'll pull the trigger."

She froze, her body rebelling against every movement her brain telegraphed. Terror seized every muscle, though shock loosed her tongue. "You're dead."

"You're not happy I'm alive?" Mitchum arched an eyebrow and smiled. "Not very Christian of you, is it?"

"We heard them shoot you." She kept her eyes on his face, away from the gun that wanted to rob her of her sanity. As the fear ebbed, the rational part of her mind fought. She needed to keep him talking, distracted. Maybe one of the men across the parking lot would figure out what was happening before he could take her. Or worse.

"You heard a nice piece of theater." Keeping the gun leveled on Ashley, Mitchum pulled the door open and slid into the seat, careful to keep the weapon below window level. "I wasn't even at the hospital when we fired that shot."

So Ethan had been right. Ashley kept her eyes on Mitchum's face as she tried to breathe evenly. "You were trying to run us where there were no witnesses."

"Very good. We needed a way to protect my cover and still get to you, but no matter what I did, Kincaid wouldn't leave you alone with me. The whole hospital plan would have worked and both of you would have been out of the way before he could report my death, but there went Kincaid again, off the plan, doing his own thing. This all could have been over two days ago. Your cousin could still be alive, if Kincaid had done what he was supposed to do."

"You killed Katrina?" Bile rose and mixed with raw anger, choking out the last of her fear in white-hot rage. This man, who'd sat in her hospital room and chatted with her like an interested friend, who'd spent months beside Ethan, gaining his trust… This man had brutally, horribly, taken her cousin away—was likely about to do the same to her. Without caring about the consequences, she threw a punch, catching him square in the jaw.

He'd grabbed her by the wrist before she could take advantage of his surprise. Mitchum worked his jaw from side to side, his gaze coated with derision. "I did what I had to do." He shifted in the seat, angling to keep the weapon squared on her.

"Why?" The ache in Ashley's fist and the nonchalant coldness in the man's gaze tamped her emotions into weak shadows, but fear still taunted her. "Why kill for these men? Why betray your country?"

"Because they pay better than the government ever could. Now, start the vehicle and drive before our friends over there figure out I'm supposed to be a dead man. I've got some people who want to pick your brain."

Ashley balled her hands and shifted her feet. She wasn't moving this vehicle an inch if she didn't have to. But then her heel caught on the corner of the laptop on the floorboard. Reaching for the steering wheel, hoping to keep Mitchum's eyes on her hands, she slid the laptop under the seat with her foot. For now, their information was safe, but she couldn't stall much longer. *Lord, make one of the men turn around. Get Ethan here. Do something.*

"So you want to move slowly?" Mitchum stopped smiling and leaned closer, jamming the gun into her side very near to where the first bullet had left its scar. "Will that help you pick up the pace?"

Ashley winced, hot fear racing across her skin and tightening her muscles, but she refused to make a sound. She swallowed hard against welling panic, trying to focus on the moment, the moment she'd feared most in life. There was no way to escape this, but she'd already lived with fear and dealt with death. There wasn't much more he could do to her.

In defiance of her temporary bravado when she'd hit him, the sight of the weapon paralyzed her. "I can't. Not while I can see the gun."

Tapping his finger against the side of the weapon, Mitchum regarded her for a moment then seemed to decide she was telling the truth and lowered the gun between his seat and the door. "With Turner in custody, you aren't necessary anymore except as a way to leverage him. If you try anything, I'll kill you and we'll find another way to find out what he knows."

Alive. If she could stay alive one more minute, there was hope. It was all she had. Minute by minute.

Clicking her seat belt into place, Ashley reached forward and turned the keys Ethan had left in the ignition, half hoping the Jeep wouldn't start.

It purred to life.

She shifted into gear, praying she could remember how to drive a stick. It had been years. "Where?"

"You just take the turns as I tell you and you'll be fine. And if you try anything…wrecking the car, driving to a police station, calling out for help at a stoplight—" Mitchum pulled a cell phone from the leg pocket of his tactical pants "—I will call and have Turner killed in your place."

Ethan pulled his helmet from his head and dropped it onto the floorboard, slumping in his seat. The rest of the team piled into the Suburban, looking no less defeated than he felt. He dragged a hand down his cheek, palm scratching on several days' worth of stubble. At least the men behind him didn't have to look into Ashley's eyes and see the hurt there, hurt already squeezing in his own chest. They'd failed Sean.

He'd failed Sean. It was his phone call that had set this into motion. His phone call that was likely intercepted in time for Sean's captors to move him.

Klass stayed outside, talking into his mike before he climbed into the driver's seat and stared out the windshield. "It gets worse." He started the vehicle and looked at Ethan, then at the rest of the men. "Surveillance saw Mina go into his office, but when our guys went in, he was gone. His whole staff, computers, everything. Gone."

It couldn't be possible to deflate even more than he already had. Ethan balled his fists. "He's bolted."

"We've got a team headed to his house, but I'm sure it'll be empty, too." Klass shifted the van into gear. "We slipped a tracker onto his vehicle when he pulled into the parking lot, but it hasn't moved. It's still sitting right where he left it."

"So how'd he get out of the building?" James spoke up from where he sat suffering from an obvious adrenaline crash.

"A truck from an office-supply company in town, First Class Supply, came to the rear for a delivery about an hour before Mina arrived. We're looking for the truck. Otherwise, I have no idea."

"What now?" one of the other men called.

"We retrieve Ms. Colson, get her to safety and wait for orders."

The plan sounded good to Ethan. In the wake of bitter disappointment and heightened concern about Sean, all he wanted was to lay eyes on Ashley and to see for himself she was still safe.

The moment they turned the corner onto the street where they'd rendezvoused with the team, his remaining hope crashed. The Jeep was gone.

Klass flashed him a look and floored the SUV to the spot next to the remainder of his team, slamming on the brakes and bringing the truck to a skidding halt.

Winters approached as Ethan jumped from the vehicle and ran around the front, heart pounding. "Where's the Jeep? Where's Ashley?"

"Your partner showed up with orders to move her to a more secure location. He grabbed a radio from the van to stay in communications then left with her."

Ethan's grip on his rifle tightened as his pulse accelerated. "Mitchum was killed two days ago. I passed the information up last night." But he hadn't been able to reveal Mitchum had been working for the wrong side, which made news of his purported death low on the priority list. He should have said something, should have warned the team. If he had, Winters would have been ready for the threat.

"News hasn't made it to us yet." Klass walked away, speaking to one of the communications techs. If Mitchum had a radio, that meant all of their communication as a team was subject to compromise.

Ethan didn't have time to wait for backup plans and orders. Every second ticking by was one last second Ashley had. "Which way did they go? When?"

"Not even five minutes ago. Headed south." Winters looked stricken, his face tight. "I'm sorry. I had no idea."

"Not your fault." Ethan spun and scouted the area. South. Away from Mina's office and his house. Toward the suburban area on the outside of town.

Klass stepped up. "What do you think, Kinçaid? She's your charge, but with us on radio silence, anything you do has to be on your head."

"What was the name of the office-supply company?" It was a long shot, but it was the only lead they possessed. If Mina had taken off in one of those trucks, then it was likely he had contacts in that business and a safe place to hide.

Klass spun a hand in the air. "Load up."

The team scrambled into the Suburban.

Klass grabbed Ethan's arm. "We'll find her."

Not trusting his voice, Ethan simply nodded and pulled away, slamming the door to the SUV behind him. He just prayed it wasn't too late when they did.

TWENTY

There had been ample opportunity to call out to other drivers, to run the Jeep into power poles, any number of ways to escape on the drive to the back of a shopping center several miles from where they'd started. But always, more than the gun in Mitchum's hand, Ashley was aware of the phone and its power to end Sean's life. Somewhere on the drive, she'd passed panic and fallen into something even darker, that space where her emotions died and she could no longer feel at all.

"Stop here."

Ashley pulled up behind a loading dock and wrested the Jeep into Park, leaving the engine running. It was a slim advantage, but it was something.

Keeping the gun hidden, Mitchum pressed a button on the phone and pulled it to his ear. "I'm here." He listened, frowning. "How long before you arrive? We need to end this and get out of town." Flicking an angry glance at Ashley, he punched the end button on the phone with his thumb and shoved the device into his pocket.

"Your partners disappoint you?" She couldn't help it, couldn't stand to be silent and defenseless in front of the man who'd killed her cousin and betrayed the man she loved.

"Shut up. And when I come around, step out." He got out of the Jeep, holstering the gun, and crossed in front of the vehicle before Ashley could move fast enough to put it in gear and hit him.

She shut off the engine and slipped out, hands away from her sides, praying the laptop was too far under the seat for him to spot. Shutting the door as quickly as she could, she wished she hadn't disabled the Wi-Fi and GPS. It hadn't made a difference anyway, and it might have helped Ethan to find her now.

"Up the stairs and through the door. We'll wait in the back for them to get Turner here and finish this."

The brick building was long and low. A loading dock for what appeared to be a store ran along the back. "Where are we?"

"Near the public. So if you run, I will put in the call to end Turner. Then I'll walk out front and find someone else to die in your place."

A spark of fear burned through her dead emotions. Not only was Sean's life in her hands, so was the life of some innocent shopper searching for bargains on a spring morning. There was nothing she could do. Nowhere she could turn. Once again, nowhere she could look but up.

And she would for as long as blood pumped through her veins.

The door squeaked as Mitchum pulled it open, ushered her inside and slammed it shut, sinking the small room into darkness before he flicked a switch and flooded the room with light.

They were in some sort of small office, dusty and likely unused. An old desk sat in the corner, a metal chair with a ratty plastic seat shoved to the side.

Mitchum nodded at the chair. "Sit." He surveyed the

room and cursed. "Nothing to tie you with, but I doubt you'll be much of a problem."

Sinking into the chair, Ashley prayed he'd keep the gun out of sight. At least then she could pretend it wasn't there. With it hidden, the rational part of her mind could focus.

She surveyed the room. She could probably make the door, but there was nowhere to run for cover, and she doubted she could start the Jeep and pull out before Mitchum got his bearings and fired. Even if she did, he still had the power to deal death to others. Death that would be all her fault.

Mitchum stared her up and down. "I told Kincaid you were trouble, that he ought to back off this case. He should have listened. Without him, you'd have eventually led us to the drives and we could have just taken them without having to get you involved. It would have looked like a petty theft. Turner's disappearance would have been written off as an insurgent uprising. Nobody would be the wiser and you'd be home right now, doing whatever thing it is you do. But no. Kincaid just had to be your hero."

The more he talked, the longer she lived. "Why do this? Ethan said you're a good man, a good agent."

"Like I said." Mitchum crossed his arms and leaned against the wall. "They pay better than the government. They made me an offer before I ever came into the unit, and I took it. Helped me pay off some debts, buy some things I had my eye on." He sniffed. "Living the American dream."

"By destroying everyone else's dreams. Who's your partner inside?" If he'd tell her who the other mole was, she might be able to find some way to leave a message for Ethan, some way not to let this all be in vain.

Mitchum laughed. "I'm the only one. Kincaid got careless. It's amazing what you learn by bugging a guy's pickup. You told me every move you were making." He checked his watch, glanced at his phone, then returned to staring at her. "I can see why Kincaid's got a soft spot for you. You don't back down easy, no matter what anybody says. You're not hard to look at, either, are you?"

Ashley's eyes narrowed, panic slicing through her core. There were fates worse than death, fates she'd never let herself consider before. She was dealing with a man who'd proved human life held no value, and there was no telling what he'd do to her if he thought it would break Sean.

Outside, the sound of an engine hummed and died, nearly stealing the last of Ashley's hope. With the arrival of reinforcements, her clock was ticking down.

Mitchum straightened and looked at his watch again. "That was quick. And once Turner talks, this will all be over. Your only worry is how long it will take him. It could get—"

A second engine. Squealing tires. A shout.

Gunfire.

Ashley shrieked and ducked, covering her head as bullets flew outside, cracking against the walls of the building.

Mitchum dived, taking cover behind her, gun pressed to the back of her head.

Above it all, the loudest sound was her own breathing, broken and erratic, pacing faster as her skin burned. She wanted to run, but if she moved, Mitchum would pull the trigger. She was trapped, one unbroken cry repeating in her mind. *Jesus, Jesus*.

The door burst open and a man appeared, a broad-shouldered silhouette against the late-morning light, rifle barrel sweeping the room. He took a step farther in, eyes familiar behind the goggles under his helmet.

Ethan.

Of all the times in her life she'd ever needed him to appear, this was the most desperate. If she could, she'd go straight to him and never leave. Only the threat of death held her back.

He let the door swing shut behind him, his jaw set in a hard line, anger sparking from his eyes as he focused on the man behind her, though he didn't aim his weapon. He couldn't, not without putting her into his direct line of fire.

Mitchum jammed the gun harder against Ashley's skull, the metal cold and threatening, channeling fear so overwhelming it stripped away every other thought and turned her muscles to water. "Get up."

She struggled to stand, slipped to the chair.

He grabbed her under the arm and hauled her up, but the barrel never wavered.

Ethan didn't flinch, eyes hardening. "Mitch, there's an entire team outside making short work of the men you were supposed to meet. It's over."

Mitchum's fingers dug into Ashley's arm. "No, it's not. I'm going to walk out the front of this building, and if you follow me I'll kill her and any civilian that gets in my way."

Ethan's trigger finger eased closer to its mark. "You know I won't let you."

Ashley needed to find a way to stay calm, to keep her mind rational. Focusing on the moment wouldn't do it. Reaching for Ethan was impossible. There was only one place to look. The control in this situation wasn't hers, wasn't Ethan's, wasn't Mitchum's.

God, get us out of this.

Peace calmed her mind. Like the last time, the world revolved slower, seconds stretching longer as her thoughts centered on her next actions.

Ethan would never fire as long as she was between him and Mitchum, whose agitation had him likely to go off at any moment. The only thing to do was to get out of the way.

Staring hard at Ethan, she willed him to look at her. When his eyes flicked to her face, she glanced away. Before he could acknowledge the motion, she gathered all of her reserves and dived sideways, flinging her hand back toward Mitchum's weapon, praying it would be enough.

The gun slipped from behind her head and went off twice by her ear, deafening her to the world and to the scream she knew ripped from her throat, the report so loud it overwhelmed her senses until she couldn't even see.

Mitchum's iron hold on her arm tightened and jerked her back as her vision cleared.

Ethan lay on the floor, clutching his bloodied right thigh.

Ashley wanted to scream, to fight, but emotion clogged her throat. She whipped around and threw punch after punch, fists connecting ineffectively over and over.

"Knock it off." Mitchum shoved her to the cement, the impact grinding her jeans against her knees and dragging the skin from her palms.

Scrambling for Ethan, Ashley ran a hand over his chest, looking for more blood, found it leaking from a graze to his right biceps and seeping through his fingers on his leg.

"I'm okay." The words were tight with pain, but Ethan's gaze was clear and steady.

They were both alive—for the moment.

Ashley scrambled for some way, any way, to save them both, but nothing came through. All she had was the irrational need to tell Ethan she loved him before they both died.

"Back away from him." Mitchum stepped closer, gun menacing a silent threat. "Now."

Ethan deliberately met her eye then looked down at his uninjured leg, repeating the motion twice.

Ashley followed his gaze as Mitchum stepped closer.

Strapped to Ethan's thigh was his SIG, too far for him to reach quickly, but right by her hand.

She swallowed hard, met his eyes in panic. She hadn't touched a gun in five years, was terrified of the weight of one in her hand even now.

Ethan's gaze moved from the gun to her to Mitchum and back again. He gave her a slow nod.

"I said move. You're as dead as he is if you don't clear the path. I'll take the heat for taking you out." Mitchum raised his weapon.

God, help me. Anything she needed to do was out of her control. There wasn't time for Ethan to lean forward and unholster his weapon. Ashley had to do this and she had only one chance. With one last prayer and every inch of her willpower, she forced frozen muscles into motion.

Her hand shot forward and ripped the weapon from its holster. As the cold weight of the metal rested in her hands, Ashley rolled onto her back, raised the pistol, steadied her hand and fired.

Everything went into motion at once.

The echo of the gunshot bounced off the walls and pounded against Ethan's ears. The sound waves pounded into his aching ribs, pulsing pain in time with his heartbeat.

Mitchum's gun slipped from his fingers and clattered

to the floor as he bellowed in pain and staggered backward, a dark stain spreading across the shoulder of his shirt.

Ashley scrambled to her feet, gun unwavering in its aim straight at Mitchum's heart. Her face was set, jaw tense, body like a statue.

Fighting past the pain in his chest and leg, Ethan pushed himself forward, grabbed Mitch's weapon and knelt to take aim, the weight on his good leg. He leveled the pistol as the door flew open, bouncing against the wall behind him and showering the room in daylight.

Men streamed in around him—at least six—filling the small space to capacity, separating him from Ashley. Still, he didn't lower the weapon until Mitchum was fully subdued.

The instant the threat was neutralized, pain kicked into full gear, his chest throbbing with an intensity he hadn't imagined. Passing the gun to one of Klass's agents, Ethan braced a hand against the wall and held on, willing away the ache that intensified with each breath. He would not pass out. Ashley needed him.

Fighting for shallow breaths, Ethan regained his equilibrium and pulled himself up, using the wall for support, resting heavily on his uninjured leg. His eyes found Ashley's across the small room, and she gave him a small, sad smile.

Before he could get closer to her, Klass stepped between them, his expression dark. "You shouldn't have broken away from the rest of us, Kincaid."

Ethan refused to back down. "If I hadn't, Ashley would be a hostage or dead." He'd never apologize for coming for her, even if the action cost him everything he had.

Klass exhaled loudly then shook his head, the edges of his expression softening. "Can't say I ever thought I'd see the day when you'd let your heart rule your head, but it was probably the right thing this time." He stepped to the side and braced an arm around Ethan's lower back, urging him toward the door. "Let's get you downstairs. I want my medic to take a look at you, maybe put you in the ambulance when it gets here, make sure you didn't crack a rib and puncture a lung."

"I'm fine." Ethan wanted to pull away, wanted to go to Ashley, but his injuries robbed him of his fight as Klass and another agent braced him on either side and helped him limp toward the door.

"You might be fine, Kincaid, but you're needed outside."

As they stepped through the door, sirens wailed in the distance. Sunlight reflected off the government SUVs and a white delivery truck. Ethan blinked at the glare and shook off his help, determined to make it down the steps under his own power. "What about Ashley?"

"I want her in that room until we cart Mitchum and the rest of the group off the premises."

Ethan nodded. It was better for her not to see the men who would have killed her had Klass and his men not arrived when they had.

When the team had pulled into the lot, all of Ethan's focus had been on the Jeep, parked by the back loading dock. All he knew from that moment was Ashley was in the building and needed him. He'd been halfway to the door when the delivery truck screeched in and the shootout between the team and Mina's men ensued. How he'd made it into the office without getting hit was a blessing that could only be attributed to God.

"Was Mina with them?" *Please, God.* If he wasn't, this was far from over. Ashley would have to go into witness protection, and Ethan would have to pursue the case. The likelihood of seeing her again dwindled, slowing his steps. He needed her. And if he was forced to leave his job and go into WITSEC with her, he would. Without hesitation.

Klass stepped aside to let an agent in full gear pass them on the stairs. He looked hard at Ethan then toward the small parking lot a few steps below them. "He was in the back of the delivery truck." Pointing toward two SUVs turning onto the main road, he said, "That's him and his guys being hauled away now. Our men will take them in and work with your unit to put this thing to rest once and for all."

Ethan wanted to breathe a sigh of relief but his lungs wouldn't let him. "And Sean Turner?"

"He's still in the truck. We'll move him when the ambulance gets here." Klass laid a heavy hand on Ethan's shoulder. "He's pretty banged up."

Using the stair rail for support, Ethan took the steps as quickly as he could and headed for the white truck sitting just past the loading dock. He'd never been so relieved to have his feet on solid ground in his life as he limped toward the truck, where a medic worked on someone whose face he couldn't see.

When the medic moved to the side, Sean caught his eye, gave a quick, pained smile and said, "Aren't you a sorry sight?" Bruises swelled the side of his face, highlighting the blue in his eyes. His lips were swollen from what had to have been repeated blows. Pain etched deep lines around his mouth, but he was alive.

Ethan grabbed the high bumper of the truck, relief weakening his muscles. "Not half as sorry a sight as you are." In spite of the pain, he couldn't stop the grin. Mina was in custody. The mole was revealed. Sean and Ashley were safe. "You okay?"

Arching an eyebrow, Sean shifted painfully, wincing as the medic concentrated efforts on his shoulder. "I'm still breathing. Ask me later if I'm okay."

Ethan's smile faded. Sean might be alive, but he'd clearly endured much at the hands of his captors. There was no way to tell what they'd done to him. "I'll be praying."

Nodding, Sean let his eyes drift shut, then opened them again, focusing on something over Ethan's shoulder before coming back to him. "Don't let Ash see me yet. She's been through enough."

"She'll beat me down to get to you." It was true. Once she heard Sean was safe, Ashley wouldn't let anything stop her from seeing him with her own eyes.

"I'm sure you can find a way to distract her." The lines on Sean's face softened and he tipped his head toward something over Ethan's shoulder. "You know she's been in love with you for years."

Ethan glanced back. Ashley stepped out the door, flanked by two of Klass's agents. Even from this distance, the shaking in her hands was obvious, but she was safe.

One foot stepped toward her. Then Ethan stopped, caught between his friend and the woman he loved. Some part of him still couldn't stop thinking of her as Sean's, couldn't stop wondering how Sean felt about any of this. He turned back to the truck.

"Break her heart and I'll come after you, Kincaid." Sean lifted his hand and waved toward Ashley. "Go to her. She needs you."

Ethan hesitated.

Laying his head back against the side of the truck, Sean closed his eyes. "Go, before I decide you're too much of a wimp for her."

Reaching into the truck, Ethan squeezed Sean's uninjured shoulder, then stepped back, walking as fast as his aching side would let him.

Ethan met Ashley as she stepped off the last step. Her face was pale, but she smiled softly when she saw him. He held out one arm to her and she stepped into his embrace, pressing her face into his shoulder, avoiding his injured side. He wished with everything in him that he could pull her tighter against him.

He dipped his chin, burying his face in her hair, soaking in her warmth. "You okay?"

Ashley nodded. "Are you?"

"Yes. And so is Sean."

Pulling away slightly, Ashley looked up at him. "Where is he?"

Ethan released her and laid his palm against her cheek, slipping his fingers into her hair. He scanned her face, reveling in just looking at her. "He's being looked over by the medics, but I promise you he's okay. You can see him at the hospital."

Ethan let his eyes drift to her mouth and back up again. His thumb traced her bottom lip, sending electricity into his fingers. Everything was over, and he could let his guard down. All he wanted was to kiss her, to tell her with his actions what words weren't adequate enough to say.

She nestled against his palm. In all the years he'd known her, she'd never looked more beautiful. Everything in him ached for her, but now wasn't the time. As much as he wanted to, he still couldn't supplant God in her life. It would be wrong.

But God knew how much he loved her.

Sirens grew louder as two ambulances rounded the corner into the parking lot.

Planting a kiss on her forehead, he whispered into her

hair. "They're going to make me get in the ambulance." He pulled back, trapping her gaze. "Then there will be debriefings and interrogations and…" His words trailed off into nothingness at the look in her eye. *Forget it.* He couldn't help himself. "I love you."

"And I love you." She eased away, resting her hand on his shoulder, her fingers brushing his neck. "Because I want to. Because God put us together and He'll take care of the rest."

Nothing he'd ever heard in his life had ever been so incredible. Slipping his cheek next to hers, he waited to see what she'd do. At the slight turn of her head, he pressed his lips to hers, following her lead as she deepened the kiss, speaking things his heart ached to hear, pouring herself into him without restraint, without reservation.

Without fear.

EPILOGUE

Ethan had never been so scared in his whole life.

"What exactly are we doing out here again?" Ashley tromped through the woods behind Ethan, her hand warm on his back as he led the way on the narrow path, boots nearly silent on the carpet of spring growth. The sun dappled in the northern Virginia sky, the June air cooler in the shade.

She'd asked him five different times since he'd parked the truck, and each time he'd changed the subject. His heart hammered harder in his chest every time for fear he'd say the wrong thing and tip his hand too soon.

In the two months since Craig Mitchum and Sam Mina had been taken into custody, Ashley had grown more like her old self every day.

Ethan felt his lips curve. Including being as pushy as ever. He could live with that if it meant he had his Ashley back, the woman who faced the world head-on, refusing to back down even to him. She still had her moments, still had those times when she crawled inside herself, but now that she'd faced her worst nightmare and won, now that she'd surrendered control of her life to One higher than herself, those days were fewer and farther between.

"Are you going to tell me?" Ashley pressed harder against his back, urging him to talk.

"That makes the sixth time you've asked. No. Why don't you tell me about your meeting this morning?" When she'd called to say she'd be late, the excitement in her voice nearly reached through the phone and tweaked his own emotions. "New client?"

Her hand slid up his back to his shoulder, pulling him to a stop as she stepped behind him.

Ethan held his breath. If she stood any nearer, he'd kiss her and tell her everything before he was ready. His feet stuttered to a halt. They were so close to making this perfect. He'd never forgive himself if he jumped the gun now.

Ashley leaned forward, her breath brushing his ear and sending warmth straight into his stomach. "I took on a whole new job."

"What?" He spun on one heel, his grand plans sinking through his fingers to the leaves on the ground beneath him. "Where?"

Ashley's hand dropped from his shoulder as she took a step back and smiled wickedly at him. But then something over his shoulder caught her eye and her smile slipped in confusion. "Ethan." His name was barely a breath as she stepped around him.

He let her go, enjoyed watching the look on her face as she stepped into the clearing, the Rappahannock River opening up in front of them.

"What is this?"

The answer to the question hinged on her answers to his next two. "Where's your new job?"

Ashley turned back to him, blond hair slipping over her shoulder, coy smile edging up. "Close."

"Close to what?"

"To you."

It was almost impossible to breathe. The distance between them for the past two months had been tough, but they'd handled it. "You're moving here?"

"Better." She threw her hands out to her sides. "I'm contracting with your unit. Seems there's a need for a consultant, someone on the outside with my specific skill set. The colonel said you could use a solid computer-security expert with a law-enforcement background." Her grin widened.

Ethan wanted to pull her to him and kiss her breathless, but he held himself back and crossed his arms over his chest. "You'll need a place to live."

Her eyebrows knit together, probably because he wasn't doing the very thing he wanted to do. "I can get an apartment."

"How about here?" He swept his hand toward the clearing behind her.

Ashley shook her head, opened her mouth, shut it again.

Forget it. He couldn't not touch her any longer. He stepped forward, wrapped his arms around her and pressed his forehead to hers. "Here. We'll build a house. Together. This could all be yours." He pulled her closer as he tilted his head back to see her face. "But only if you'll marry me." His heart raced so hard, she had to feel it.

Her smile broadened. "Yes."

He wanted to tease her, wanted to ask her if it was because she needed him or because she wanted him, but he didn't get the chance. She kissed him. Hard. With all of the emotion he knew she possessed. All of the emotion that had been unlocked in her since she'd surrendered her life to God…and her heart to him.

* * * * *

Dear Reader,

I am so honored you came along on this journey with Ethan and Ashley! Thank you, thank you!

Shortly after I graduated from high school, I was diagnosed with a panic disorder. It was a ten-year ordeal that sidelined my original college plans, spiraled me to the edge of depression and changed the course of my life. Looking back, though, I see where God took the bad and used it for my good in amazing ways. To be honest, while I would never want to endure those years again, I am grateful it happened because it made me who I am today. It also gave God the chance to prove in 2001 that He really is my healer!

For a long time I've wanted to write a novel where the hero or heroine suffers with debilitating fear. While Ashley's PTSD is situation-specific, there are many people in the world who have been gripped with fear that affects their everyday lives. It's impossible to explain to others what is happening to you and, often, that can drive a person into a pit of low self-esteem. I urge you, if this is you, to seek help. Even more, I want you to know you are not alone. When I finally spoke up, it was amazing to learn how many people just in my own circle had silently suffered, also. Believe me…there is no shame and no judgment when it comes to asking for help.

I pray for those of you who know what panic feels like. While it may sound like an easy answer, it is true God is always there, even when the road is rough. In the midst of those ten dark years, there didn't seem to be any light. When I look back today, I see God's fingerprints everywhere. Start looking for Him. I guarantee you'll find Him.

Thank you again for spending your valuable time with Ethan and Ashley. If you want, you can always visit me at www.jodiebailey.com and drop me a note!

Jodie Bailey

COMING NEXT MONTH FROM
Love Inspired® Suspense

Available September 1, 2015

THE PROTECTOR'S MISSION
Alaskan Search and Rescue • by Margaret Daley
As an Anchorage K-9 police unit sergeant, Jesse Hunt regularly puts his life at risk to rescue others. But he'll pull out all the stops when a bomber threatens his hometown—and his former high school sweetheart...

RODEO RESCUER
Wrangler's Corner • by Lynette Eason
Tonya Waters isn't about to fall for another cowboy bull rider, yet when handsome Seth Starke offers help escaping her recently freed stalker, she'll accept. She barely eluded the assailant before, and now he's after Tonya *and* Seth.

PLAIN THREATS • by Alison Stone
Ever since her husband's crimes left Rebecca Fisher an Amish widow, she's been targeted. To discover whether her stepson knows more than he lets on, Rebecca turns to his professor for answers. But the questions put them *both* in danger...

DESPERATE ESCAPE • by Lisa Harris
Former special ops agent Grant Reese is trained to defuse land mines—not rescue damsels in distress. But when Dr. Maddie Gilbert is kidnapped by drug traffickers, he'll face any threat to save the woman who's always held his heart.

EASY PREY • by Lisa Phillips
US marshal Jonah Rivers has never forgotten his brother's widow, Elise Tanner. When he finds her in a dire situation—with a nephew he didn't know existed—he'll stop at nothing until they're both out of harm's way.

EXPERT WITNESS • by Rachel Dylan
Tasked with protecting a sketch artist who is testifying in a high-profile murder trial, US marshal and former FBI agent Max Preston jumps into action to keep Sydney Berry safe. But can he save her from the secrets of her past?

LISCNM0815

REQUEST YOUR FREE BOOKS!
2 FREE RIVETING INSPIRATIONAL NOVELS PLUS 2 FREE MYSTERY GIFTS

Love Inspired® SUSPENSE
RIVETING INSPIRATIONAL ROMANCE

YES! Please send me 2 FREE Love Inspired® Suspense novels and my 2 FREE mystery gifts (gifts are worth about $10). After receiving them, if I don't wish to receive any more books, I can return the shipping statement marked "cancel." If I don't cancel, I will receive 4 brand-new novels every month and be billed just $4.99 per book in the U.S. or $5.49 per book in Canada. That's a savings of at least 17% off the cover price. It's quite a bargain! Shipping and handling is just 50¢ per book in the U.S. and 75¢ per book in Canada.* I understand that accepting the 2 free books and gifts places me under no obligation to buy anything. I can always return a shipment and cancel at any time. Even if I never buy another book, the two free books and gifts are mine to keep forever.

123/323 IDN GH5Z

Name _____ (PLEASE PRINT) _____

Address _____ Apt. # _____

City _____ State/Prov. _____ Zip/Postal Code _____

Signature (if under 18, a parent or guardian must sign)

Mail to the **Reader Service**:
IN U.S.A.: P.O. Box 1867, Buffalo, NY 14240-1867
IN CANADA: P.O. Box 609, Fort Erie, Ontario L2A 5X3

**Are you a current subscriber to Love Inspired® Suspense books and want to receive the larger-print edition?
Call 1-800-873-8635 or visit www.ReaderService.com.**

* Terms and prices subject to change without notice. Prices do not include applicable taxes. Sales tax applicable in N.Y. Canadian residents will be charged applicable taxes. Offer not valid in Quebec. This offer is limited to one order per household. Not valid for current subscribers to Love Inspired Suspense books. All orders subject to credit approval. Credit or debit balances in a customer's account(s) may be offset by any other outstanding balance owed by or to the customer. Please allow 4 to 6 weeks for delivery. Offer available while quantities last.

Your Privacy—The Reader Service is committed to protecting your privacy. Our Privacy Policy is available online at www.ReaderService.com or upon request from the Reader Service.
We make a portion of our mailing list available to reputable third parties that offer products we believe may interest you. If you prefer that we not exchange your name with third parties, or if you wish to clarify or modify your communication preferences, please visit us at www.ReaderService.com/consumerschoice or write to us at Reader Service Preference Service, P.O. Box 9062, Buffalo, NY 14240-9062. Include your complete name and address.

*Can K9 cop Jesse Hunt help Lydia McKenzie unlock her
memories to catch a serial bomber?*

Read on for a sneak preview of
THE PROTECTOR'S MISSION,
the next book in USA TODAY *bestselling author*
Margaret Daley's *miniseries*
ALASKAN SEARCH AND RESCUE.

Lydia closed her eyes and tried to relax. But visions of
the bombing assailed her mind. The sound of hideous
laughter right before the bomb went off. The expression on
Melinda's face when she knew what was going to happen.
Was she alive? The feeling of helplessness she experienced
trapped under the building debris. Her heartbeat began to
race. A cold clamminess blanketed her.

Her hospital room door opened, pulling her away
from the memories. When Lydia saw the person who
entered, her pulse rate sped faster. Jesse Hunt. She wasn't
prepared to see him.

He looked as if he'd come straight from the crime
scene. As a search and rescue worker for Northern
Frontier, he'd probably work as long as he could function.
The only time he'd rest was when his K9 partner, Brutus,
needed to.

So why is he here?

He stopped at the end of the bed. "Bree told me you
were awake, so I took a chance and came to talk to you."

His stiff stance and white-knuckled hands on the railing betrayed his nervousness, but his tone told her he was here in his professional capacity. Saddened by that thought, Lydia said, "Thank you for finding me."

"I was doing my job yesterday."

"Knowing the people who would be searching kept my hope alive. Have you found everyone?"

"We don't know for sure. Names of missing people are still coming in. I was hoping you could tell me how many people were in the restaurant when the bomb exploded."

"I don't know…" The thought that the bistro was totally gone inundated her. She dropped her gaze to her lap, her hands quivering. Emotions crammed her throat. She turned for her water on the bedside table, but it was too far away. She started to lean forward and winced.

Jesse was at her side, grabbing the plastic cup and offering it to her.

She took it, and nearly splashed the water all over her with her shaking.

Jesse steadied the cup, then guided it to the bedside table. "I know this isn't easy, but anything you can remember could help us piece together what happened. We've got to stop this man."

"Nobody wants that more than me. I'm sure I'll remember more later." She hoped she could.

She needed to.

Don't miss
THE PROTECTOR'S MISSION
by Margaret Daley,
available September 2015 wherever
Love Inspired® Suspense books and ebooks are sold.